Fit For Treasons

Henry James Garon

DEDICATION

For my father. I miss him.

CONTENTS

Acknowledgments   i

1   Does Not All Commands   1

2   Very Poor Indeed   17

3   Beasts Shall Tremble   35

4   We Are Such Stuff   49

5   The Fume Of Sighs   65

6   Surfeit With Too Much   81

7   Glorious To This Night   101

8   Time Is Broke   119

9   That Perilous Stuff   133

10   King Of Infinite Space   149

11   Fit For Treasons   165

ACKNOWLEDGMENTS

My dad was a Hollywood publicist, and a big fan of Rod Serling. When my dad was still in school, he worked with Rod Serling at one of the networks, and he prevailed upon Mr. Serling to speak at his graduation. I watched re-runs of *The Twilight Zone* many times growing up, and I always wanted to write those types of stories. I guess I inherited my love of Rod Serling from my dad. So thanks to Rod Serling and my dad.

Thanks to my mother for reading stories to me when I was a toddler. Thanks also to my mother and my brother Johnny for helping me to edit these stories. Thanks to Johnny, and my brother Joey and his wife Beth for all of their love and support. Thanks to all my family for all of the laughs and all of the fights over nothing.

Thanks to Mike McCarthy for all of his advice.

Thanks to my friend Dave Gerry who fixed my printer for free.

Thanks to all the many people who write blogs giving advice on how to self-publish, how to fix your computer, and how to cool off a beer really fast.

And thanks to God, who invented me out of whole cloth.

1 DOES NOT ALL COMMANDS

Every good servant does not all commands:
No bond but to do just ones.

It was twilight in the early summer of 1935, and a new power line ran along a paved road that wound through the center of Adamsville, nestled in the forests of northern Georgia. But hopes of greater glory had diminished somewhat after the local bottling plant lost its franchise, and most of the townsfolk drifted elsewhere.

The town had one gas station, a barbershop and a grocer. At the corner, where the business route met the other paved road, stood the tidy two-story building owned by the L'Oiseau Drug Company. The drugstore was closed, but the proprietor, Abraham L'Oiseau, could be found if you followed the other road north for about a half mile after it ceased to be paved.

There was no doctor in town, but L'Oiseau, the druggist, was reputed to be the smartest man in the territory. Abraham L'Oiseau and his son settled in the two story Victorian house a few years ago, when he set up business, paying cash for both properties.

Word spread that L'Oiseau was a widower, and his

somber mood confirmed to all that he was still grieving. Any distrust of the druggist soon faded after it became known that L'Oiseau was very keen at his trade. He could prepare remedies that would make folks better, without charging a lot of money.

As darkness enfolded the home, the light streaming out of the windows on the garage became more distinct. It was more of a laboratory than a garage: the walls were lined with all sorts of gadgets and powders, wires and tools.

Abraham L'Oiseau, graying and bearded, with wire-framed spectacles, looked old enough to be the grandfather of his 10 year-old son, Isaac. Isaac was fair-haired and slight, weighing only 60 pounds, which worried his father sometimes.

Both father and son were staring intently at a table made of lead. There were several coils of wires running from the table to two Tesla coils and an array of vacuum tubes. There was nothing on the surface of the table, except for an apple.

"Now, you might want to go stand a ways over there son. I don't know if this is safe for you."

"Okay Dad." Isaac walked a few paces away, behind a windowed panel. Both were wearing the same leather apron, which covered Isaac front to back and top to bottom. Both father and son pulled down their welding visors.

Abraham threw the switch on the control panel in front of him, and immediately the area surrounding the apple became distorted, as though it were being viewed through an unseen lens. There was a loud hum and a few slight crackles from the electricity. Abraham looked back and forth from a timer to the table, and then closed the switch after ten seconds had elapsed.

"It worked!" Isaac squealed.

"But the apple is still there," Abraham said.

"But it worked. I saw it move a little bit. Didn't you?"

"I don't know, son. My eyes aren't as keen as yours. Anyway, it's not supposed to move. It's supposed to go forward in time."

"Well maybe it did go to the future, but just a little bit," said Isaac hopefully.

"I don't know." Abraham removed his glasses and wiped his eyes. "It's late. Time you were going to bed."

"But Dad, there's no school tomorrow. It's summer."

"I'm not going to have you staying in bed all morning. School or no school, you get up early like me."

Isaac repeated the gist of the age old proverb: "'Cause that's when you get all the wisdom."

"That's right. Now you get along while I clean up in here."

Abraham kissed his son goodnight, and the boy hung up his leather apron and visor as he left the garage.

The night was filled with the sounds of crickets and forest birds, and Abraham was deep in thought. He walked over to a chalkboard that had a series of equations, absently picking up a piece of chalk as he did so. Abraham stared at the equations, and then sat down at a nearby desk and opened a large notebook of graph paper. The notebook was filled with notations and sketches of the machine with the lead table. He pulled his pipe out of the drawer and lit it. Time passed.

The door to the garage opened, and Isaac walked in wearing his pajama bottoms and a t-shirt. His face was expressionless.

"What's wrong son? You have a bad dream?"

"No," Isaac said. "I know what is wrong. Your son was right about the time machine working. The problem was that you didn't gauge the distance properly. You only sent the apple ahead one moment in time."

Abraham squinted at Isaac through a cloud of tobacco smoke. "What are you getting on about boy? You *are* my son."

"Yes, I am. But I am speaking to you from the future. Your son is asleep, and when he fell asleep I was able to possess his body to speak to you. I am Isaac, but I have come from the future where you sent me."

"I sent you to the future?" Abraham asked.

"Yes."

"When?"

"I can't say, unless you promise to do everything I tell you."

Abraham normally drew the line at any sort of sass-talk from Isaac, or any other little boy, but there was something about the boy's detached expression that made Abraham resist the urge to take Isaac over his knee.

"Promise you why?"

Isaac's face had a blank expression. "We must not allow the events that led to my present existence to be changed. Otherwise the incongruity will cause a shift in the field, and the circuit will be broken."

"Boy, are you playing at some nonsense with your old man?"

"No. I will show you how to properly gauge the distance, but first you must promise to do everything I say."

Abraham was nearly dumbfounded at this unexpected turn, but he had no idea of any other option. "I promise," he heard himself say.

"Swear."

"Okay, then. I swear."

Isaac walked over to the chalk board, picked up the chalk, and began to write. "The problem here is that you don't have the proper means of measuring out intervals of time..."

Isaac erased bits of the equation and wrote in other bits as Abraham watched. Abraham had only taught his son the very basics of algebra and geometry, but this boy was correcting equations of differential calculus. Abraham watched quietly and began to worry about his son.

The next evening found a new gauge wired up to the table. Abraham set the gauge to one minute as Isaac looked on.

"So what you saw last night was actually a slight shift in the continuum," Abraham said. "Do you remember?"

"Yeah, I remember, Dad. Why do you keep asking me that?"

"Because it was right before you went to bed, and sometimes you get tired and forget things."

"No, I remember that fine," Isaac said. "I saw the apple move a little bit, and then you sent me to bed."

"And that's it?"

"Yeah, Dad. That's it. Don't you remember you sent me to bed?"

"Yes, I do. I guess I was tired too. Anyway, after you went to bed we figured out that we needed to measure the distance of time more accurately."

"Who's we, Dad?"

"Well, I guess I felt like I was working with you even though you were asleep." Abraham stepped away from the table. "Okay, son. Go stand back a bit."

Isaac went back to where he stood the night before, and both pulled down their visors. Abraham opened the switch. As before, the area surrounding the apple was shifting and unfocused. Then the apple disappeared.

Abraham closed the switch.

"It worked! You did it!" Isaac danced around joyfully while Abraham continued to stare at the table. Abraham glanced at his watch.

"*We* did it son. You helped me, remember?"

"Shucks, Dad. You did it all. I just saw it shift a little bit last night."

"That's right, son. But you helped me more than you know."

Abraham continued to look at the table, and check the time on his watch. Isaac noticed this and stood still, and then turned to look at the table.

The apple reappeared. Isaac leaped into the air. "It worked! It worked!

An hour later, Abraham was sitting in his comfortable chair, reading a book and taking notes. Isaac came into the room wearing his pajamas.

"What's wrong, son? Can't sleep?"

"It is me again. Isaac is asleep."

"But I thought you were Isaac."

"Isaac is a little boy. I am a grown man. To me, Isaac feels like a different person."

"I see," Abraham said.

"I have come to see that you will hold up your end of the bargain."

"And what does that entail?" Abraham asked.

"You have given your oath, so you must not try to evade your duty. You are known to be a man of your word."

"Get to it, son. What must I do?"

"Tomorrow, Caul McGillis will ask your son to go hunting with him and his father. You are to let Isaac go."

"How's that?" Abraham heard a tone of anger in his own voice.

"You gave your word."

"I know that Hiram McGillis is a dangerous fool. I'd never let Isaac go hunting with him."

"It must be so," Isaac said. "Events that have happened cannot be altered or the circuit will be broken."

"If I let Isaac go hunting... Then what?"

"Then these events will come to pass, as they already have for me..."

Abraham saw things transpire in his mind as the boy described what was to happen.

"The boys will go hunting with Hiram McGillis..."

Abraham had a vision of Isaac and Caul McGillis as they walked behind Hiram McGillis. Both boys were towheaded, the same age and size, wearing heavy flannel shirts against the morning chill. Hiram carried a rifle and watched closely for any motion in the woods.

Hiram stopped and took a nip from a flask. He heard a motion in the underbrush. Hiram raised his gun and took a bead at something moving in the fog. He fired.

"Isaac will be sent to retrieve the game, and ... there will be an accident."

Hiram nodded his head at the boys to fetch the game that Hiram just killed. The boys scrambled off.

Hiram took another hit from the flask, and heard something else. He quickly aimed and fired. There was a cry of pain!

Abraham felt his face grow hot and flush. Beads of sweat began to form on his forehead and underarms. But he continued to listen to the boy describe the future events, and he watched them unfold in his mind as though he were having a nightmare.

"Hiram will take Isaac to you to see if you can save the boy."

Abraham saw Hiram and Caul rushing towards the house. Then Hiram was standing on the porch, holding Isaac in his arms, while Caul banged on the door.
Then Abraham saw a vision of himself in his nightshirt, silently examining the still body of his son.

"You will realize that there is nothing you can do to save your son..."

Abraham wanted to tell the boy to shut up, and to stop him from saying any more. And yet he desperately wanted to hear if there was any hope.

"There are people in the future who know how to save a boy who has been shot..."

So that was it! That was why this entity had helped Abraham to fix the time machine. Abraham saw himself taking Isaac into the garage and laying him down on the lead table. In his vision, he set the gauge and pulled the lever...

But all that was yet to happen. Abraham was still sitting in his comfortable chair, watching his son Isaac standing before him in pajamas.
"What do you say, Abraham?"
Abraham heard himself talking. His voice sounded calm. "I don't know what to say. You want me to send my son off hunting with that fool McGillis so's he can get

killed?"

"You gave your word," Isaac said.

"I know what I said, and I know what you said. But this is foolishness. There are some men who should not be trusted with weapons, and Hiram McGillis is one of those men. I never let Isaac go hunting with McGillis. That man doesn't know when to cork up a jug."

"You know Hiram McGillis hasn't your means. He hunts only to provide for his family. He has paid you many times with wild game that he shot."

Abraham's gaze had drifted to a Bosch print that was over his desk, where a man in a tall black hat was performing tricks for a crowd. Abraham cast a sidelong glance at the boy.

"So he has," Abraham said.

"You know there is danger, and you know there will be harm. But you also know the cure. Isaac will be sent to the future. You know this is possible."

"And then what?"

Isaac held up his hands. "Am I not proof? I come back in his stead. And you will have me always with you. Think of it: Right now you have no guarantee of Isaac's safety. But with me, you have. I have told you the future, and so it will come to pass. What do you say?"

Abraham thought carefully for a moment. "I will send the boy to the future as you wish."

"And the hunting trip?"

"I will give Isaac permission to go hunting." Abraham said.

"Good. It will work out for the best. You will see."

The boy headed back to his bedroom, leaving Abraham alone in his chair. Despite the warmth of the evening, Abraham felt a slight chill.

The next day found Abraham behind the counter in

his store, filling a prescription. The bell over the door rang out as Isaac and Caul McGillis ran in. Abraham looked down his glasses at Isaac, who stopped at once.

"Hey, Caul. Can you wait outside while I talk to my dad?"

"Sure, Isaac." Caul ran outside as Isaac sheepishly approached the counter.

"Hey, Dad, I wanted to ask you something."

Abraham continued working. "What is it son?"

"Well, I know how you never let me go hunting with Mr. McGillis on account of…"

"Because he is reckless?"

"Yes. Well, you see, Caul was saying that Mr. McGillis doesn't drink as much as he used to. And Caul says that Mr. McGillis is more safe now on account of he doesn't drink as much…"

"Yes." Abraham was still looking down on his work. He closed his eyes for a moment.

"Well, I was wondering … since Mr. McGillis is a safer man now, if you would let me go hunting with Caul and Mr. McGillis Saturday next. I promise I'll be careful."

Abraham came around the counter and squatted down to eye level with Isaac. "Are you sure you want to go, son?"

"Yes, Dad. I'll be careful. You know I will."

"Yes. I know you will. I love you son. You know I would never do anything to hurt you. And you know I've always tried to look out for you. Your mother isn't with us anymore, but I've always tried to do my best by you."

"I know you have, Dad."

Abraham embraced Isaac tightly. "You're all I've got son. I don't want to see you ever get hurt. I would rather hurt myself than see any harm come to you."

"I know that, Daddy."

"Your mother and I didn't think we could have children, and then when we had you, we felt that you were a special gift. Your mother was so happy. You were her greatest treasure. And when she died, I promised her I would look after you. And I've always tried to do that."

"You look after me really good, Dad."

Abraham gazed intently at the eyes that Isaac had inherited from his mother. "I'm going to say that you can go, but you've got to promise you'll be careful."

"Gosh Dad, thanks. I'll be careful. I know I will."

Isaac hugged father and ran out of the drugstore before Abraham would have a chance to change his mind.

Abraham looked after Isaac for a second and then slowly rose, and walked back behind the counter.

That evening, Abraham was in his chair, smoking his pipe and reading a book. Isaac came down the stairs, and Abraham looked up from his book.

"Yes, son?"

"It's me again, Abraham."

"I thought as much," Abraham said.

"You've given the boy permission to go tomorrow?"

Abraham fixed a hard gaze on the boy. "Yes. As I said I would."

"It will work out for the best. You shall see."

"I'm hoping you're right," Abraham said.

The boy turned to go back upstairs.

"Listen son, there was just one favor I wanted to ask of you."

"You want to make sure the time machine works?"

"No, I've already tested that. It's just that I worry about what the boy will feel tomorrow …. The pain."

"It can't be helped. That is part of the deal."

Abraham stood up and walked over to his kitchen

counter. "Well that's just it. I'm a druggist, you know, and we deal with remedies for pain."

"Yes?"

Abraham pulled out an envelope of powder and a glass.

"You see, I was thinking about the pain that Isaac would feel tomorrow. I thought of a remedy so that Isaac won't have to suffer."

Abraham poured the powder into the glass, added some water and mixed it up. Abraham handed the glass to the boy, who made no move to take it.

"And you want me to drink this?"

"Please. As a favor to an old man who doesn't want his child to suffer."

The boy took the glass. "Very well."

Abraham watched him drink the mixture. The boy handed the glass back to Abraham. "There. I guess that's all that needs to be done. I'll bid you good-night then."

"Good night, Isaac."

"Good night, Abraham."

Abraham watched Isaac walk back upstairs.

The next morning there was a knocking at the door. Abraham answered the door in his bathrobe. Hiram McGillis was at the door holding the boy. His face was pale and his voice shook. Abraham could smell liquor on his breath.

"It was an accident. I was facing the other direction and I heard a noise."

There was a lot of blood. "How bad is it?" Abraham asked.

"I don't know if he's alive. I ran as fast as I could. You've got to help him."

As the stranger had foretold, Abraham laid the body

of the boy down on the table and set the timer. Abraham and McGillis put down their visors. Abraham pulled the lever.

The body disappeared for a moment, and McGillis gasped. The body returned after a moment. McGillis and Abraham rushed over to the table to see if the boy was alive. Hiram looked down into the sleeping face of Caul McGillis. Abraham checked the pulse. Abraham shook his head.

McGillis collapsed in grief over his son. "My boy. I'm so sorry. I killed my own son!"

"You didn't mean to." Abraham said.

A few days later, Isaac and Abraham were walking together through the cemetery.

"Gosh, Dad, I feel so sorry for Mr. McGillis. He feels awful about shooting Caul like that."

"It's a tragedy son. It couldn't be helped."

Isaac thought about this for a second, and looked around to make sure no one was listening. "Mr. McGillis said you tried to help Caul by putting him on the table in the garage..."

"Yes."

"So does Mr. McGillis know about the time machine?"

"I didn't tell him it was a time machine. I just told him it might help Caul."

"But it didn't help. Did it?" Isaac asked.

"I don't know."

Abraham and his son walked on for a moment in silence.

"Dad, you know I can't help but wonder if that might have been me that got shot if I hadn't of overslept that day."

"I don't even want to think about it," Abraham said.

"It's kind of fortunate that I overslept then, I guess."

"I guess it was."

"That was really strange. I just couldn't wake up that morning. I felt so tired I couldn't open my eyes. I didn't even wake up until noon that day."

"Yes. You were very sleepy," Abraham agreed.

"Do you think maybe that Mom was looking after me, and that was why I overslept?"

"I think your mother is always looking over you son."

They came to a small pond and continued on the path around it. "So you didn't get to go hunting," Abraham said.

Isaac waved his hand. "Aw, that's alright."

Abraham was watching Isaac as they walked. "And McGillis didn't give us any game."

Isaac looked up at Abraham in surprise. "You know we never eat anything that McGillis shot. Neither one of us like squirrel or raccoon or possum. We always put it in the garden. You said you only take it so that McGillis' pride won't get hurt. And you told me never to tell Caul, and I never did."

"No, I guess you never did." Abraham looked up at the power line that ran along the main road to town. "Isaac, when you talk to me, what do you call me?"

"I always call you 'Dad'."

"You never call me by my name?" Abraham asked.

"You said a son should never call his father by his Christian name. You said it's disrespectful."

"Even when you're older?"

"I don't know why that should make a difference. You'll always be my dad."

Isaac reached out and held his father's hand.

"Even when you're grown?" Abraham asked.

"Even when I'm grown up."

Abraham patted Isaac's head gently as they continued

walking toward their house.

Later in the garage, Abraham knelt in front of the machine with a screwdriver, undoing the bracket that held down a wire harness. He heard the door squeak behind him, and Abraham turned around to see Isaac in his pajamas.

"I knew you would destroy it now," the boy said.

"You're back?"

"Yes, but you should know that, after you destroy the machine, I cannot come back. It was a temporary ... door."

Abraham continued working. "That's what I figured."

"Tell me, how did you know that I was Caul McGillis and not your son?"

Abraham didn't answer.

"It doesn't matter. I should have known I couldn't fool the smartest man in Adamsville."

Abraham continued to dismantle the machine.

Caul continued: "Let me tell you that I meant no harm. I only wanted the chance to live out my existence here."

Abraham had begun unplugging the wires.

"Listen. It won't be long now. I must be going. You've kept your son safe, Abraham. He's lucky to have you for a father."

The boy suddenly fell over, and Abraham rushed to catch him. Isaac was breathing normally. He was still asleep.

Abraham lifted Isaac up and carried him back into the house.

"I've got you, son. I've got you. Everything's going to be all right."

The End

2 VERY POOR INDEED

"Who steals my purse steals trash; 'tis something, nothing;
'twas mine, 'tis his, and has been slave to thousands;
But he that filches from me my good name
Robs me of that which not enriches him,
And makes me poor indeed."

There was only one seat left at the counter, and Liz took it. The man sitting just to her right moved his newspaper out of her way. "Sorry," he said. "I'm all over the place this morning."

Liz smiled at the man. "That's fine," she said. The man was thin, and slightly pale. He wore a new suit, and his face seemed to shuttle back and forth from confidence to nervous trepidation.

The man started arranging his newspaper in a pile at his elbow. Liz saw him take a deep breath, and hold his face in his hands, moving his lips and muttering. She thought she recognized him reciting snatches of a positive affirmation. Or perhaps he was praying.

The man gestured towards the paper. "You can read this if you want, but I'll warn you: There's not a lot of good news in that paper today."

"Thanks for the heads up," she said.

"Sure." The man took another deep breath. "I'm trying to stay positive today. I've got a job interview, and ... well, it's just good to stay positive. You know?"

Liz looked up from her menu. "Well, good luck. I'm sure you'll do fine."

They smiled at each other for a moment. The man looked away. "I hope you don't mind my bothering you. I get less nervous when I'm talking to someone."

"That's fine. I hope you don't mind, but what sort of a job is it?"

The man reached into his breast pocket and pulled out a large wallet. He unfolded the wallet, took out a card and handed it to Liz. "They design circuits. I'm an engineer. I used to..." His voice trailed off.

"What?" Liz was curious by nature, and she couldn't bear it when people didn't finish sentences.

The man took another deep breath. "I was going to say that I used to have my own company. But I don't anymore." He paused. "I'm not a very good businessman, I'm afraid. But I'm trying to stay positive this morning."

Liz made the sign of a fighting fist. "That's the stuff," she said, smiling. Liz looked down at the card, just as the waitress came by with the man's bill. The man put the money and tip down on the counter just as his phone rang. He looked at the number on the phone. "Excuse me, I have to take this," he said.

The man took the phone call outside. It was over very soon, and he was smiling when he poked his head back in the door. He waved to Liz. "Good news, but I've got to be going. Wish me luck."

"Good luck," she said. She turned back to the menu, smiling to herself, and the man was gone down the street.

Liz had begun eating her breakfast, and she started leafing through the newspaper that the man had left behind. That was when she noticed that he had left his wallet on top of the paper. She took the wallet and dashed out of the coffee shop. Liz was rushing down the sidewalk, looking for any sight of the man, when she stopped.

"What am I doing?" She said to herself. "He's long gone by now."

Liz started back into the coffee shop and saw the waitress going through her purse.

"Hey! That's my purse! What are you doing?" she said.

The waitress sounded very casual for one who was apologizing. "Sorry. I thought you ran out on the check." Liz didn't trust the waitress.

Liz took back her purse and paid her check. She started to explain. "No, I was trying to catch someone who left. He left ..." Liz had started to hand the wallet to the waitress, but then she thought better of it. She put the wallet into her purse. "He left in such a hurry. I didn't get a chance to say goodbye."

"Better luck next time," the waitress said.

Later, Liz was walking down the street, holding the wallet in one hand while she talked to her friend Georgia on her phone. "I didn't want to leave it with Ms. Grubby hands. She seemed a little too comfortable going through other people's stuff."

"Look who's talking, Ms. Lost-and-Found." Georgia said. Georgia had gone to school with Liz, and now she was working in a credit card call center. Georgia was supposedly a top earner as a salesperson, but Liz had often wondered how this was possible when Georgia was always talking to Liz on the phone.

"I'm just going to return Mr. ..." Liz read the name on the driver's license. "Douglas Lazarre's wallet to the address on his license. How hard could it be?" Liz said.

"I have a feeling this is going to turn out just like that kitten you rescued from the pound," Georgia chided her.

"His wallet is going to die from distemper?" Liz said.

"You know what I mean."

It was a normal stucco house in a McMansion neighborhood. Liz knocked on the door. A man in a bathrobe answered.

"Hi. I'm looking for Douglas Lazarre?"

The man looked askance at Liz. Perhaps she had interrupted his TV show. "He doesn't live here. I just bought this place a couple months ago."

"Oh. I see. You don't have a forwarding address, do you?"

"I'm sorry." The man shut the door.

Liz started away from the door, and heard a voice from behind the neighbor's trellised hedge. "I know where he is."

Liz stopped, and spoke to the hedge. "What?"

"I know where Mr. Lazarre is," the neighbor said. "I saw the whole thing happen."

Liz walked over to the hedge. Liz could faintly make out the neighbor's face from between the star jasmine. "Lazarre's in jail," he said. "I saw the whole thing. The police arrested him and took him away. He was dealing drugs."

Liz remembered earlier in the coffee shop, when Douglas had told her that he used to have his own *company*. 'Yeah,' Liz thought to herself. '*Pharmaceutical* company.'

"That's what we don't need in this neighborhood is a

bunch of drug dealers," the neighbor said. "You know what I say? Good riddance."

Liz was in her car, talking on the phone with Georgia. "I told you this was not a good idea," Georgia said. "This guy is a criminal, Liz. You don't know what you're dealing with."

"I know. But I've got to get his wallet back to him, even if he is a criminal. You know why? Cause if I didn't, that would be *stealing*."

"So what're you going to do?" Georgia asked.

Liz opened the wallet. "There must be some other identification."

On the other end of the line, Liz could hear Georgia's nail file, hard at work. "Are you going through his wallet?"

"Well how else am I going to find out where he lives?" Liz said.

"You are so nosey," Georgia said. "What's in it?"

Liz pulled out a slip of paper. "A ha!"

"What is it?"

"A piece of paper with an address on it," Liz said, reading the paper. "And I'm just a couple blocks away!"

"Get out of town!"

"And it says Friday at 10 am. What time is it?"

"Just a second." Liz heard Georgia shift to check her watch, and then she heard a paper cup spill over.

"Quarter till. Ooops!" Georgia said.

"What's wrong?" Liz asked.

"Nothing."

Liz was pulling into a parking lot. "Okay. I'm here. Call you back."

Liz walked through the mini-mall, holding the paper and looking for the right store front. She stopped in front of a sign that said '*The Serenity Shop*'.

Inside was a small meeting room with chairs laid out in a circle. A gray haired man was in the back of the room, pouring himself some coffee.

"Excuse me. I'm looking for Douglas?" Liz said.

"I haven't seen him yet, but he's usually here on Fridays. Have we met?" The man held out his hand. "I'm Tom."

"I'm Liz. I'm a ... friend of Douglas's." Liz noticed more people coming through the door and taking seats around in the circle.

"I'm a friend of Bill W's." Tom said.

"Does he know Douglas?" Liz asked.

Tom looked at her a moment. "We're getting ready to have a meeting. You're welcome to stay."

"Thank-you," Liz said. She quickly sat down, nodding and smiling to the other people.

A man opened his notebook and read from the first page: "Welcome to the Friday morning meeting of Narcotic's Anonymous. I'm Fred, and I'm a Meth Addict."

Everyone but Liz said, "Hi Fred."

Liz felt embarrassed.

A while later, Liz was in her car in the parking lot, talking on the phone.

"So he's a felon and a drug addict?" Georgia asked.

"That's not supposed to be any of my business. It's supposed to be anonymous." Liz said.

"It's all right, Liz. You didn't mean to pry. It's just that you were going through his wallet ...."

"Well what am I supposed to do?" Liz said.

"Uhm, find some more stuff?" Georgia suggested.

"I can't. It just gets worse."

"Well, how else are you going to find him?

Liz let out a big sigh. "Okay." She opened the wallet again and pulled out some items. "A business card. A photo of a lady."

"His wife?" Georgia asked.

"He's not married." Liz said.

"He told you that?"

"He's not wearing a ring."

"Oooh." Georgia paused. "You looked at his ring finger. Liz likes the bad-boy type."

"Georgia!"

"What else is in his wallet?"

"A little girl's photo," Liz said, looking at the photo. "She's adorable." Liz turned the photo over. "Oh, both of these photos were done at Sam's. That's right up here on Laurel. I could see if they have his new address."

"This is like a detective movie."

Liz started her car. "Okay. I'm headed out."

"Call me back."

Sam's was a little photo studio. Most of the space was devoted to a three light set-up with blue background. One side-wall was covered with cubby-holes that were filled with props. The walls around the shop were decorated with the head-shots of dozens of actors. Some of them were famous celebrities.

Liz scanned the head-shots and found the same photo of the lady that she had seen in Douglas's wallet. Liz held the little photo up to the big one.

A voice behind her said, "Can I help you?"

Liz turned around to see the man who had appeared behind the counter. "Yes, you can. I'm looking for..." Liz looked at the name on the bottom of the head-shot. "Andrea... Uhm..." She pointed at the photo on the wall. "Her! Did she leave you a forwarding address?"

The man behind the counter nodded. "She sure did.

Andrea gets a lot of work from that shot."

"She doesn't have a last name?" Liz asked.

"Nope. Just Andrea. You know actresses. Marketing." The man was looking through his register. "There it is. Andrea. I'll just copy the number for you here."

"Could you give me her address too?" Liz asked.

"I don't see why not. She has it on her resume. There you go." He handed Liz a slip of paper with the address on it.

"Thank you so much."

"Is this for a soap opera?" he asked.

"Kind of."

A short time later, Liz was knocking on Andrea's apartment door. A beautiful strawberry blond actress, answered the door. She was wearing an exercise outfit.

Andrea smiled. "Yes?"

"Hi. I wanted to ask you about Douglas Lazarre?" Liz asked.

Andrea opened the door for Liz. "Douglas? Sure, come in."

Liz followed Andrea into her living room.

"I just got back from working out, so pardon the mess," Andrea said.

"I'm sorry to barge in on you."

"Well, I'm really surprised to be hearing about Douglas. We broke up *months* ago." Andrea walked over to the refrigerator and pulled out a bottle of juice. "Mango juice?"

"No, thank-you." Liz noticed the many pictures of Andrea that adorned the living room.

"We only dated a short time. It was just one of those things. Two different worlds, really. I mean, he's like a technical kind of guy."

"Because he's an engineer?" Liz asked.

"Is that what he told you?"

"Well..." Liz hesitated.

"Yeah. He told me that too. But he works at odd jobs. He doesn't hardly make any money." Andrea took on the tone of one making a logical demonstration. "I mean if he's an engineer, why doesn't he make more money? It didn't make any sense."

"Maybe he couldn't find a job." Liz offered.

"I guess. But there's another part of it. I think he's been in jail. I remember hearing something about the department of probation on his answering machine."

"Oh?"

"Yeah. I just didn't want to get involved with ... a felon, you know?"

Liz nodded. "I guess."

Andrea caught sight of herself in the mirror, and couldn't resist primping. "It was sad because ... This is going to come out wrong, but he was just crazy about me."

"He was?"

"Yeah," Andrea said. "Well, maybe not about me. About the way I *look*. I look like his ex."

"He was married?" Liz asked.

"Yeah. I guess she split. He didn't like to talk about her. You know some guys: No personal stuff."

"Yeah. You don't have his current number?"

"No. Sorry. I like to make a clean break and move on. I've had three different boyfriends since then."

Ten minutes later, Liz was walking on the sidewalk outside the apartment, talking to Georgia over the phone and making fun of Andrea.

"*'I've gone out with three different guys since then.'* She really said that?

"Can you *believe* her?" Liz asked.

"I have a tiny waist and men love me," Georgia said. "Don't hate me because I'm beautiful."

Liz laughed, but then quickly sobered. "Of course, it does confirm that he's been in jail."

"You're going to *believe* that cow?" Georgia asked.

"No. But I looked in the wallet again and found another business card." Liz admitted.

"Oh? What is it?"

"His probation officer."

"Oh."

Liz read from the card. "Manuel Ortega. Department of Probation." There was a pause. "I don't want to do this anymore. I mean it started out like an adventure, but now he's just..."

"Yeah, I'm with you, sister. This guy is starting to sound creepy."

"What should I do?" Liz asked.

"I think if you find a wallet, you can just throw it in a mailbox and the post office will return it," Georgia said.

"Is that true?"

"I don't know." Georgia admitted.

"Where did you hear that?"

"I'm not sure. Just try it. What've you got to lose?"

Liz noticed that there was a blue mail collection box near the corner, just in front of where she was walking. Liz took the wallet out of her purse, and started walking toward the box.

"I knew it would be like this," Georgia said. "This is just like the kitten."

"How is this like my kitten?"

"Well, you had to put that kitten to sleep. Now here you're having to put the wallet into the mailbox. That's like putting it to sleep. Kind of. You're putting that guy out of his misery. Or your misery."

Liz opened up the mailbox door, and then hesitated. "How is mailing a wallet like putting a kitten to sleep?"

"Oh, never mind, Liz. Just do it. Drop him in the mailbox and have done with it."

Liz closed the mailbox. "I can't do it. I put that kitten out of its misery, not mine."

"What difference does it make?" Georgia asked.

"I don't know. I started this and I'm going to finish it." Liz opened the wallet again. "Where's that probation officer's card? *He's* probably got an address, right?"

"Yeah. But those places are kind of skeezy. Isn't there some other place you could go?"

Liz found the white card with the state seal on it. "I'm running out of options here.... And how do you know that those offices are skeezy?"

"I had that DUI, remember?" Georgia said.

"Oh yeah."

Liz didn't think that the neighborhood was that skeezy, but the probation office itself was. She soon found herself sitting across a desk from Officer Manuel Ortega, who was a little overweight and had a gray goatee.

"Look, Miss..."

"Poirot," Liz said.

"Poirot, I sympathize with you, but I can't give you any personal information from Mr. Lazarre's case."

"I'm not asking for personal information," she said. "Just his address and phone number."

Ortega scratched his chin. "I don't know. If anything happens, it's on me."

"But I'm trying to help him," Liz said.

'You'd be surprised how many people end up having to see me because they were trying to *help* someone."

"What do you mean?"

"Take, Mr. Lazarre...." Ortega paused. "No, I

shouldn't discuss this."

Liz hated it when people started sentences and didn't finish them. "Please, you were saying?"

Ortega got up and closed the door to his office, and then sat down again, and leaned across his desk, speaking in a low tone. "He shouldn't even be here, in my opinion. Mr. Lazarre got a raw deal."

"What do you mean?"

"Look, I get the cases after they're finished. I see a lot of people. Mostly criminal types. I handle drug dealers. That's my department. Well this guy, Lazarre, comes in here and I'm looking at his record: *Nothing.* This was his first offense. He doesn't say he's innocent, but he never says he's guilty. He's very careful with what he says, like he asked his attorney what he had to say. And he just takes it, without complaint."

"So he's stoic," Liz offered.

Ortega shook his head. "No, it's more than that. I start wondering about this guy, so I check out his case with the DA."

Ortega looked up at the frosted glass walls to see if anyone outside of the office was in earshot. Then he continued in a low voice. "I have a friend at the DA. He tells me about the case. It turns out that Douglas, Mr. Lazarre, has a brother. His brother was a drug dealer. I should say he *is* a drug dealer. He's got a *long* record of dealing everything. They think Lazarre let his brother move into his home. A little later the DEA found out they were using the mail to move drugs around."

"So why didn't they arrest the brother?" Liz asked.

"They didn't have any proof that the brother was living there. They arrested Mr. Lazarre because they thought they could get him to drop a dime on his brother."

"But he wouldn't talk?"

28

Ortega shook his head. "Not a peep. Like I said: he's very careful with what he says. Mr. Lazarre knew that his brother had two strikes on him. If he went up on this charge, that would have been life."

"So what happened?"

"Mr. Lazarre didn't crack. He took the rap." Ortega paused for a moment. "I hope his brother appreciated that."

"So he went to jail?" Liz asked.

Ortega nodded. "That's right. He took a plea: Served one year and got five years of probation."

"That's terrible."

"Ain't it, though? And he's not a bad guy, Mr. Lazarre. I think I'm a pretty good judge of people. He's a good egg."

Liz paused. "So does that mean you're going to give me his address?"

Ortega shook his head. "Nope. But look: I'll make you a deal. I'll tell you where you can find him. It's a public address, so there's no trouble." Ortega wrote down an address on a card and handed it to Liz.

"He'll be at this address tonight at 5:30."

Liz stood up and shook his hand. "Thanks, Mr. Ortega."

"Sure, and if you see Mr. Lazarre tell him... Better not. Just don't tell him anything, okay?"

Liz nodded and winked. "Check."

Liz was soon back in her car, talking to Georgia. "So that's it? You're going to drop it off tonight?"

"I don't know," Liz said. "That's one option, but I had another idea."

"You found something else in his wallet?"

Liz was looking at a child's crayon drawing that she had found: it showed a Mom, Dad, and little Girl in front of a house.

"Yeah, I was thinking. There's this drawing in his wallet that his daughter did."

"Okay..."

Liz turned the picture over. "Well, on the back it says "Emily Lazarre, Carpenter Elementary, Mrs. Thompson, 2nd grade."

"You're going to give his wallet to his daughter?" Georgia asked. "She's in the second grade!"

"No. If she's in the second grade then he has to pick her up at school. That means when school lets out, Douglas will be at Carpenter Elementary School."

"O-M-G. You are *sooo* smart."

"Really, Georgia. *Any* genius could have thought this up."

Liz was standing outside of Carpenter elementary school. The children had gone, and the cars and busses had gone. Liz looked around and wondered what went wrong.

The people in the office told Liz how to find Mrs. Thompson's room. It was a fairly neat class, with colorful construction paper butterflies hanging from the ceiling.

The lady at the teacher's desk had a dark complexion, and her hair was tied back in a bun.

"Mrs. Thompson?" Liz asked.

Mrs. Thompson looked up, smiling. "Yes?"

"Hi. I'm sorry to bother you. I'm trying to find one of your students. Emily Lazarre?"

Mrs. Thompson's expression went blank for a second, and then her smile did not return. "You didn't hear about her?"

"Hear? No. I'm ... a friend of her father's."

Mrs. Thompson shook her head. "Oh, that poor

man. It was three years ago. They were such a nice family. Jennifer, his wife, used to help out at the school." Mrs. Thompson's voice broke, and she paused for a moment. "There was an accident. Jennifer was driving. A truck ... hit the back end of the car. Emily was killed."

"Oh."

"It was awful. Emily was such a great kid. Smart. Always cheerful." Mrs. Thompson gazed out the window, as if her memories lay outside on the playground. "And then she was gone."

For a moment, Mrs. Thompson was overcome, and paused before continuing. "Then I had to tell the class. Try telling a second grade class that... that..." She stopped again. "We sent them flowers and cards. But it was really difficult for them. Jennifer was a wreck. She came to the school once, but after that she just stayed in their home. Mr. Lazarre kept working. That's the way a lot of people deal with things... They just go on. It was about a month after that we heard the news about Jennifer."

"She left him?" Liz asked.

Mrs. Thompson looked at Liz. "Oh my dear. He didn't tell you. Jennifer killed herself. That's what the coroner said. About a month after the accident. Pills. I guess she blamed herself for the accident."

Liz shook her head. "He... he didn't tell me. I just thought..."

Mrs. Thompson shook her head. "That poor man," she said.

That evening, in the Tecumseh Memorial Gymnasium, two lines of boys were running drills, each line taking a turn doing lay-ups. Douglas was getting the rebounds and passing the ball to the next boy in line.

Liz watched the practice from the doorway for a few minutes before making her way sheepishly toward

Douglas.

A boy missed a lay-up and Douglas said, "Nice try Howard. Follow that one up!"

The boy picked up his own rebound and shot it in the basket.

"Good job!" Douglas said. The boy smiled and ran back into line.

Douglas noticed Liz, but he continued with the drill.

Liz held out the wallet as she approached. "You're a hard man to find."

Douglas took the wallet. "You've got to know where to look. Thank you for returning my wallet."

He started to open the wallet and take out some money. "Here, let me give you something for your time."

Liz held up her hand. "Oh, no. Please... it was my... I just wanted to return it to you. I didn't trust those people in the coffee shop."

Douglas shrugged. "Oh they're okay. It's just small portions."

"No." Liz paused. "I wanted to tell you that I... looked in your wallet."

"Well, yeah. That's how you found me I guess." Douglas shrugged.

Liz shook her head. "I mean, I found out about you... I know everything... I know about..." Liz started to cry. She turned away. "About Emily. And your wife... I'm sorry. I shouldn't have. I just wanted to get you your wallet back... You poor man."

Douglas put his arm on Liz's shoulder. "Hey, it's okay. Uhm, what's your name, again?"

Liz laughed. "It's Liz."

"Here wait." The children were surprised to see the lady crying. Douglas threw the ball to the next boy in line. "Andrew. Take over for me, will you?"

Douglas escorted Liz outside the gym.

Douglas waved his wallet in the air. "A lot of sad stuff in that wallet, I guess."

Liz was wiping her eyes. "You said it."

"Yeah. I was feeling pretty sorry for myself for a while," Douglas said. "I wondered, "Why me?" I didn't hurt anyone. I paid my taxes. I wanted a reason. I tried to think of a reason for what happened, like karma, or something that I did to deserve it. But I don't know why. I could never figure it out."

Douglas walked over to a soda machine. "Hey, you want a soda? I got money!"

Liz shook her head.

Douglas put some money into the machine. "I always treat myself to a soda on Thursday nights." He pressed the button and a soda dropped down. He took a sip before continuing.

"So I was thinking about it, and I decided to handle it like a math problem. You know: write it down and work it out logically. The hardest part is knowing what to ask. This is how I phrased it: Why did my life get taken away from me? And I thought about that for a while." Douglas took another sip from his soda.

"I still couldn't answer, but phrasing the question that way helped me to figure out the answer."

"What's that?" Liz asked.

"*My life;* like I owned everything in it. *My wife* Jennifer. *My daughter* Emily. I loved them a lot. As much as I've loved anything, I guess. But they didn't *belong* to me. They were just some people that I got to know in my life. And I'm grateful for that. They lived... and they died. Emily was eight. That's a short life for a kid, but those eight years were a gift. She was a *precious gift.*"

"But it's so sad," Liz said.

"Yes. But let me show you something."

Douglas lead Liz over to a window into the gym

where they could watch the boys doing drills.

"A lot of those kids are from really tragic homes. Dads in jail. Moms on drugs. Tragedy. And they're just kids. But they come here and we play. And they like me. And when a kid smiles at you, really *smiles* at you. You can't buy that."

They turned back. "I don't know if that makes any sense..."

"It's still sad," Liz said.

"Yeah, but there are bright spots."

"Like what?"

"Like I got the job today," he said.

"You did?"

Douglas nodded. "That's right. Hey, you want to celebrate with me? We could have pizza!" Douglas shook his wallet again.

Liz laughed, and then wiped her eyes again. "Okay. I must look like a mess."

You're fine," he said. "Look, I'll be done here at 7:30. I'll meet you right here. Okay?"

Liz nodded. "Fine." She started away, but then turned around and kissed Douglas. "Sorry. I had to do that," she said.

Douglas smiled at Liz and rubbed his cheek. "That's okay," he said.

The End.

3 BEASTS SHALL TREMBLE

I'll rack thee with old cramps,
Fill all thy bones with aches, make thee roar
That beasts shall tremble at thy din.

A motorcycle sped along highway 66, high up in the Rocky Mountains. Not far after the exit, the cycle slowed as the road turned into a gravel path. The path made several switchbacks as it traversed up towards what appeared to be a small abandoned cabin. The cabin had several unpatched spaces where the logs had shrunk down, and which would allow too much heat to escape in the winter. One of the windows was boarded shut. It hadn't snowed in a while, but there were still patches of snow in the shaded mountain vales and on the nearby peaks.

The rider retrieved a package from a fiberglass top-box that was fitted behind the seat, and walked to the front door. He noticed the freshly stacked cord of firewood on the right side of the cabin. He knocked on the cabin door, waited for a moment, and then knocked again.

The man who answered the door looked to be about

60, with a frail build.

"Can I help you?"

The rider held out the package, wrapped in brown paper. "I have a package here for Ed Finch?"

"I'm sorry. You have the wrong address." The man started to close the door.

"Are you sure? I drove all the way up here on my bike." He gestured back towards the motorcycle, as if to prove that he did not fly up to the cabin.

Ed poked his head out of the cabin to look out at the motorcycle.

"I'm sorry you came all that way, but there's no one here by that name."

The rider opened the package and pulled out a stun gun. "That's too bad. I'm supposed to give this to Ed Finch."

The rider grabbed the man by the hair and shocked him on the neck with the gun. The man went unconscious and fell down.

The rider spoke into a microphone on his helmet: "Finch is down. Ready to transport."

The rider took a large black hood out of the package, and pulled it over the man's head and locked the strap on the hood. Then the rider turned the man over on his stomach, and handcuffed his hands behind his back.

A helicopter quietly appeared over the cabin and set down. Two men got out and helped the rider to carry the man's body to the helicopter. The rider wheeled the motorcycle aboard the helicopter. Then the helicopter silently rose, and disappeared into the mountains.

Ed woke up and blinked his eyes. There were two beefy men that Ed assumed would be the interrogators. Both appeared to be in their late 20's: one with black curly hair and a wide nose; the other had hair the color of wet sand, and the complexion of a heavy drinker. The men were wearing loose-fitting blue slacks and long-sleeved white shirts with no tie. They were both having a cup of coffee.

The black-haired one looked over at Ed. "He's up." Then he spoke to Ed, "You were out for a while."

The other interrogator joined in the false joviality. "You needed some more sleep, huh? Been burning the candle at both ends?"

Ed looked around the room, and noticed that he was handcuffed to his chair.

Ed played along. "The old fake pizza delivery trick."

The fair-haired man was easily offended. "It worked on you, didn't it?"

Ed nodded his head toward the wall. "That's a two-way mirror. Are we on video?"

The fair one held up a small recording device. "Nope. We're getting everything on audio."

The dark-haired one looked upset, and took his friend aside. Ed could not hear what he said, but judging from the response, Ed could tell that the fair-haired man had the worse temper. "Who cares what we tell him? He's not going anywhere!"

"All right, but just let me lead, okay?" The dark one said.

"Whatever."

Both men turned back to Ed.

The dark haired one lead off. "Okay, now we can get down to business."

He picked up a folder and flipped it open. There were just a few pages in it.

"Now, Ed, your file says that you stole some things that didn't belong to you."

Ed was still being friendly. "Is that what it says?"

"That's what it says."

"And you guys are going to try and get me to tell you where I put those things."

"That's right."

The fair haired one was eager to start in with the threats. "And we can do this the easy way..." He took out a pair of brass knuckles and slipped them on. "Or the hard way."

"Are you guys supposed to be good cop, stupid cop?"

The fair-haired one started coming at Ed.

"Hey, that's enough out of you. I don't need to take any of your garbage."

The fair one slapped Ed hard. "You like that? There's plenty more where that came from."

The darker one casually eased his partner away from Ed. "Easy there, killer. We've got plenty of time for that."

Ed did not seem phased. "How much time?"

The fair-haired one did not disappoint. "Till the next shift. You slept through the first watch."

The dark one shot his friend another look.

The fair one volunteered an excuse. "So what? So he knows another shift comes on with the next helicopter."

"Shut up, Norm! Quit telling him stuff." The dark one said.

"You don't out-rank me. Besides you just told him my name, *Dan*."

Dan and Norm gave each other the hard stare, and then turned back to Ed.

Ed was cool. "I feel like I'm interrupting."

Dan spoke up. "Like he said, the easy way or the hard way."

Ed looked at Dan, and there was no hint of jesting in his voice: "How about this: You guys can walk out now, with your lives."

Dan smiled. "I think he wants to try the hard way,

Norm."

Norm cracked his knuckles and stepped in front of Ed.

Ed's voice remained calm. "Okay, but don't say I didn't warn you: if I tell you, I'm going to have to kill you. You still want to know?"

Norm stopped.

Ed continued. "Well you better grab a cup of coffee because it's going to take a while."

Norm looked to Dan, who motioned Norm to sit.

Ed's voice was casual, as though he was used to telling the story. "You guys know I was in the company, but really low level...."

About 30 years earlier, Ed spent a lot of time in remote outposts, working in surveillance. He knew all about wire taps and code breaking. He was pretty good. They would often call Ed when the regular crew couldn't handle it, and Ed was pretty reliable as the go-to guy.

But he got bored, and decided to take an early retirement.

Ed put all of his savings into a restaurant business that didn't work out so well. He spent a lot of fretful afternoons behind the counter at a mall, watching his workers standing around while they were on the clock. All the shoppers wanted pizza or Chinese food, but no one seemed to even want to try the lasagna that Ed's place was serving up. Eventually, Ed threw in the towel.

Ed was in his 50's and nearly broke. He had a younger, beautiful wife who seemed perpetually bored.

And then he got the call. It was someone from the company that he'd never heard of. That was Reardon.

"Mr. Finch, I've heard a lot of good things about you from your former employer."

"That's strange. Judging from my pay grade, I never

thought I made much of an impression in that place."

Reardon always sounded cool and jovial, like the sales guy who made it up to the top office. "Oh you did, my friend. A very good impression. Now listen, I'm building a new plant over in Utah...."

Ed thought that Reardon looked a little shifty-eyed in person. Reardon was only in his forties, but his hair was nearly white, and he was about sixty pounds overweight. Ed sat across the desk at HiveSweet Candy LLC, while Reardon explained the whole operation. It was a candy company, and he wanted Ed to be the head of security. Ed's background in surveillance was perfect for this sort of thing, and he had a nearly unlimited budget.

Ed spared nothing in setting up the security for the plant. Everything was state of the art: There were cameras that could point and zoom, and monitor all the activities in the plant. Reardon said he was very concerned about industrial espionage, so anything that was said in the plant was capable of being recorded. Ed had a budget in the millions to protect a candy factory. Such an extravagant waste of money could only mean one thing: he was working for the government again.

It wasn't long after Ed began working at HiveSweet that he met Sergy Krolic. Krolic was a very likeable fellow. He was always neatly dressed, with a nearly perfect smile. Krolic hardly ever took off his dark sunglasses.

Krolic's factory was roughly the same size as HiveSweet, and shared the little business park out in the Utah desert. Reardon and Ed were having a discussion outside the plant when Krolic came up alongside them, riding on his golf cart.

"Ed, I'd like you to meet Sergy Krolic."

Ed shook hands with Krolic.

"I was wondering when I was going to meet our new neighbor."

Reardon patted Krolic on the back. "Krolic LLP makes organisms for industrial uses. They're working on a bacteria that could eat up an oil spill... or something like that."

"Bacteria that eat oil? What if they fell down an oil well?"

Krolic smiled his perfect smile. "That's not my problem."

"Listen, Ed. I've been telling Krolic about the security you set up here, and he was interested in having you set a system up for him."

Krolic spoke up. "Only more secure."

Reardon got into the cart with Krolic. "We'll talk later, Ed."

Ed watched Reardon and Krolic drive away speedily in the golf cart, and he wondered what he was getting himself into.

Ed reckoned that Krolic LLP was another front company. But a guy has to work, and they were paying well. So he installed an even more expensive system at Krolic.

Krolic and Ed became friends. Ed's wife, Sylvia liked Krolic too. Ed noticed that Krolic made Sylvia laugh a lot more than he ever did. Krolic was a bachelor, and a super nice guy. Sylvia was always trying to set him up, but Ed knew that Krolic was the type who wanted to play the field.

Krolic was also a Company guy, so they had similar backgrounds. They never talked shop.

Ed should have been happy. He was making good money, in charge of security at two plants in the middle of the desert. Piece of cake. But something didn't sit right.

Ed found himself monitoring Krolic and Reardon. It was almost second nature: once a spy...

One thing that struck Ed as funny was the amount of protection that they gave workers at the candy factory. Everyone wore gas masks, heavy gloves and safety suits.

Both plants ran regular evacuation drills, and there were also occasional emergencies when cyanide reached dangerous levels and the whole building had to be evacuated.

Cyanide candy. That didn't sit right.

Then one day there was an accident at Krolic's lab. Krolic and Ed were wearing the heavy suits, goggles, gas masks, and gloves. There was a body lying motionless on the floor, covered by a tarp.

Ed lifted the tarp, and jumped back in horror. The lady was dead. She wasn't poisoned. She wasn't burned. There were growths on her...

They had to burn the body, and then seal the ashes in plastic.

After burning that body, Ed began to get worried that whatever Krolic was making in his factory might make its way out. There was a stream that ran through a large, sandy wash behind the plant, and Ed started poking around. He found frogs with three eyes, and arms growing out of their stomachs.

Ed took samples and made an anonymous report to the local congressman of the district.

Reardon just about went nuts. The congressman didn't investigate, but instead warned Reardon. Krolic and Ed were in the office the next day, listening to Reardon screaming.

"Gentlemen, there is a spy in our midst."

Krolic and Ed, company men, regarded one another. Krolic smiled.

The irony escaped Reardon. "Not necessarily in this room. But I have received reports from Sid Kaufman, he's our Rep. in the 2nd District, that someone has been taking water samples, and monitoring our movements. Now Ed, I don't necessarily blame you. I mean, we expected something like this. Hell, that's why we hired you in the first place. But, damn it, we're going to have to take more precaution."

Ed was above suspicion because of his background...

Norm and Dan were listening intently to Ed's story.

"So, being the head of security, I was assigned the task of bugging every phone call into the place. In order to prevent a computer theft, I also had access to every hard drive. And that is when I discovered the existence of Prometheus."

Norm was on his third cup of coffee. "Who's that?

"Prometheus was the name of the project. Its objective was something that defense departments have sought for ages: the Super Soldier."

"Like a super-hero?" Norm asked.

"Kind of like that. Imagine a soldier that can't get sick. He's impervious to gas attacks, germ warfare..."

"What about bullets?"

"He would have the power to heal at an advanced rate."

Dan wasn't having any of it. "Get out of here!"

"I'm serious."

Norm wanted to hear more. "So what were they doing?"

The HiveSweet Candy Company was basically

creating a natural resistance to germ and chemical warfare. Strains were being developed that could resist all of the viruses that originated in another sector of the Department of Defense.

There was an endless supply of soldiers to test the vaccines on. The testing was all covert. Troops were inoculated and then sent into battlefield conditions.

Ed wasn't sure if the conflicts were simulated, but the troops were sent into conflicts. And then gas bombs exploded in combat. To make sure that the inoculations would be tested, troops were given gas masks that were inoperative.

After the battle, technicians in gas masks would walk among the bodies of the soldiers. If they found someone still living, they took a blood sample.

Norm and Dan did not seem surprised by the inhumanity of the men they were working for.

"If you think that was bad, Krolic's lab was the real horror show."

"What do you mean?" Norm asked.

"Just imagine, if you wanted to test and see if you can grow a limb back. How would you do that?

"Oh…"

The next time, instead of the government, Ed alerted the media. He sent a couple packages to the local news anchors, and this got results. The next day there were two news crews trying to interview Reardon as he left the building, and one of the networks even showed up. The local news featured a story about a "Secret Army Weapons Lab".

Ed gave them enough material to write a book. But then someone from the Pentagon came to town, and the story went away. The local anchor quit his job, and the story dropped off the map. The network never ran it. The next week the local news was covering a story about a movie starlet's "Secret Baby".

"And then things got strange."
"What do you mean?" Dan asked.
"Our scientists started dying."
"From the program? In the labs?"
"Not from the program itself, but perhaps from the people running it. Suddenly our scientists got despondent, and started jumping off bridges, and slicing their wrists in the bathtub. The program had been largely successful, but instead of celebrating, our workers were killing themselves …."

Things changed at the office. Reardon got strangely quiet. He was worried, all right, but his whole demeanor changed. He didn't appear to know, or even to care about the suicides. And Krolic... Ed could never get a read on him. Krolic was always playing it close to the vest: Inscrutable.

And then came Ed's turn. He came home one night and found his house in a shambles. They must have sent a hit team to the house without knowing that Ed was out of town.

Ed found his wife in bed with Krolic. They had both been shot to death. The hit team had made a huge error. Ed didn't have much time left, but he would be safe until they found out that he was still alive. For the time being, no one was looking for him.

Getting into the lab was easy. Ed knew all the back doors.

Both programs were near completion, with the finished products in Krolic's office. Ed found several vials in a cabinet and helped himself.

Then he shut off all the sprinkler systems and wired both labs with explosives.

Ed was finished. Norm and Dan exchanged a look.

"So what did you do with it?" Dan asked.

"Do with what?"

"The formula. What did you do with the secret formula?"

Ed laughed. "Yeah, I knew what you meant. I just wanted to hear you ask me what I did with the secret formula."

Dan didn't laugh. "What'd you do with it?"

Ed was serious again. "You know, it's not too late. We can still get out of here, all of us, before the next shift."

Norm stood up and cracked his knuckles. "I can see we're going to have to do this the hard way."

Dan stood up. "I'm going out for some coffee. You want anything?"

Norm nodded toward Ed. "Get some band aids for our friend."

Dan left.

Norm towered over Ed, who was still handcuffed to the chair. But Ed did not seem afraid. "What? You're going to hit me?"

"Yup."

"I'm warning you." Ed said, just before Norm slapped him hard.

Ed moved his jaw. "Is that as hard as you can hit?"

"I'm just getting warmed up." Norm hit Ed in the face, this time drawing blood. Norm shook his hand.

Ed was barely conscious. "Now you've done it."

Norm fell to the floor, holding his hand. "Ow! My hand!"

Ed did not seem concerned. "I warned you to let me

go, but noooo!"

Norm continued to cry out in pain.

A short time later, Dan opened the door to find Norm lying on the floor. Ed was sitting up.

"What happened?" Dan asked.

Ed was calm. "I had to slap him around a little bit."

Dan bent over to look at Norm, who was quiet and motionless.

"What did you do?"

"I called your mother a whore, and so he took a slug at me."

Dan turned and punched Ed several times in the face, drawing blood. Ed was dazed.

Dan suddenly held up his hands in pain. "Ahhh! My hands."

Dan fell over.

Ed began to tell the end of the story. "What you are feeling, gentlemen, is a flesh-eating disease, created by the HiveSweet Candy Company."

The cuts on Ed's face began to heal very quickly.

"I covered my tracks the best that I could. I had the formula in the vials and a notebook that Krolic had kept. I knew the only way to keep the formula safe was in my own body.

"The injections made me sick to my stomach. It was about two weeks of injections, and then I was the final result of the Army's wildest dreams: The super soldier!"

Ed knocked his chair over and reached to Dan's shirt pocket. His hand strained against the handcuff.

"You were touching your shirt pocket earlier..."

Ed felt the key. "That's it!"

Ed pulled the key out and put it into his mouth. Then he unlocked the handcuff with the key in his mouth. With his free hand, he unlocked the other cuff.

"I'm sorry I can't help you guys. I can only kill. You see, I'm something of a monster."

Ed rubbed his wrists. "I worked for the Company because I thought I was serving my country. And they trained me well."

Ed walked over to the recording device and removed the thumb drive holding the audio of his conversation with Norm and Dan. "They showed me how to gather information." He tucked the drive in his pocket.

"And I worked hard for them. I thought I was making us all more safe, but all the Company does is make war on people. We don't make anyone safer. We just bring death."

Ed found a coat lying on a chair and put it on. He regarded himself in the one-way mirror.

"And now I carry the death inside me. I'm a walking plague."

Ed looked at the men dying on the floor. "I'm the culmination of all your work. All that you worship. I am Death."

Ed poked his head outside and looked around. There was no one. Ed pulled his coat tightly around him as he walked away from the building: a gaunt, black figure marching amidst a desolate mountain landscape.

The End

4 WE ARE SUCH STUFF

"We are such stuff as dreams are made on, and our little life is rounded with a sleep."

It was Tuesday afternoon, and I was thinking of cutting out early, when my editor, Scott, poked his head in.

"Did you read that email I sent you about the Rooftop Robin Hood?" he asked.

"Yes, I did. Was that supposed to be some kind of a joke?" That was my polite way of telling Scott what I thought of its potential as a story.

But this did not deter him. "I thought so too, at first. But it's no joke." My editor sat down across from me, and laid a sheaf of papers on the desk. "We've gotten a ton of calls and mail about this joker."

I started to leaf through the pile. "So it's some kind of a super hero type?"

"That's the angle I was looking at, but I have to check it over with Legal. We can't be seen as encouraging some sort of vigilante."

"And what exactly does he do besides catch bad guys?" I asked.

"Well, that's kind of what I was hoping you could work out. Right now..." Scott picked up the Xerox of a sketch and he started to describe this part. My editor always tries to sell me on the story before he ruins my life with it. "He wears black and he only operates at night... He's very tall, about 6'4"...uhm, very strong, muscular... Of course, he beats up bad guys in the middle of crimes... Oh, and he climbs buildings really fast."

"Does he spin webs?" I asked. You can only hold sarcasm inside for so long before it oozes out.

"I asked about that, but no webs," Scott said. "He doesn't even have ropes."

"Can he fly at all?" I said, playing along.

"I don't think so. But he apparently is quite fearless on the top of a roof. He runs around up on the roofs... How about the Rooftop Robin Hood?"

I winced. "You didn't say anything about wealth redistribution."

"Well, I'm not married to that one. If you could think of something better...

"Anything's better than that," I said. "How about the Rooftop Ranger?"

"Work on it. Anyway, I wanted to put our best man on this story. I think this is going to be huge. No one's broken it yet."

"Thanks chief." I said, kissing my evening plans goodbye. "I'll get on these numbers right away."

One of my first leads took me to a small corner grocer down in Glendale. Ignacio was only about 30, but he was the owner.

"When I got here, there was the safe forced open and change all over the floor. These guys just want the bills," he explained.

I was making notes on a steno pad. "And did you

catch the perpetrators at this?"

"Oh no. I was asleep in bed when the cops called me. I came over here in my nightshirt." Ignacio opened the back door to his office and pointed across the parking lot. "The guys who did this were tied to that telephone pole. The cops said they know those guys did it cause they have a lot of forensics."

I wanted to hear more about the vigilante. "You were saying something about the guy on the roof?"

"Yes, I was coming to that." Ignacio motioned, and I followed him out to the parking lot. "I was about here, and I heard someone moving up on the roof. I looked up, and there was a guy up on the roof of my store. It was hard to see him up there 'cause it was night, and this guy was all in black."

"Did anyone else see him?"

"Well, when I saw this guy, I jumped a little bit 'cause I thought it was another robber. So I point up on the roof to the cops. I said, 'Look officer! Who is that?'

We saw something on the roof move away very quickly. And let me tell you, this guy was big. He had arms as big as your leg. And man was he fast! It was like the devil chasing the bus!"

"And he ran on the roof?"

Ignacio nodded. "Like one of them mountain goats, or a squirrel in a tree. That man ain't afraid to fall."

I handed Ignacio my card. "Thank you so much, Mr. Jimenez. If you remember anything else, don't hesitate to call me. Now, the arresting officer on this case was Detective Parker?"

Ignacio went back into his desk and found a card. "That's right. Detective Parker." He handed me the card. "Keep it. That Parker's a big guy too. I wouldn't want to mess with him."

Ignacio wasn't exaggerating about Parker. I'm nearly six feet, and he was probably six inches taller. Parker looked like he worked out a lot in the gym. He had a shaved head, and wore a very stylish blue suit.

I knew the receptionist at the station, and she had let me back into Parker's office. "Detective Parker?"

Parker was all charm. "Who wants to know?"

I held out my hand. "Hi, Bill Dodge with the Sentinel. I just wanted to ask you a few questions about a grocery store robbery last week."

Parker resumed what he had been writing, typing with two fingers. "I put it all in the report. I didn't make the collar, I just filled out the paperwork."

"Well some things didn't make it into the report. There's a story about a Rooftop Ranger?"

Parker stopped and turned around. "Is that what they're calling him now? That's a stupid name."

"So you saw him."

"I don't know what I saw. Like I said, I didn't make the collar. When I got to the scene, the perps were already cuffed to a telephone pole."

"So he uses police cuffs?"

Parker stopped and sized me up. "That's right. Anyone can get them. You can probably order them on the internet. Are we done yet?"

"Almost. Just for the record, how tall are you?"

"6'4"."

"And your weight?"

"What, are you making a baseball card? I don't know, 240 or so." Parket patted his belly. "I gotta start doing sit ups."

"Did you ever play any college sports?" I asked.

"Yeah, fullback at Arizona. You gonna sign me up on a singles network, Dodge?"

"I'm just like you, Parker. I put all the facts in the

report."

I nodded to Parker as I left the office, and he gave me a cold stare. That's the way detectives say 'goodbye'.

My method of detective work is simple: I just assume someone is guilty very quickly. I thought that it was too convenient that Parker was the arresting officer, and also happened to be the same size as the vigilante, and something of an athlete. So I followed him.

Parker met up with some other cops for coffee. Then I watched him interview a witness. Then I saw Detective Parker go to the gym and do a dozen reps with a bar that weighed more than I did.

I guess you can only expect to follow a detective for so long before he finally catches on. I was actually following Parker down an alley in Los Feliz, and he disappeared around a corner. I waited for a moment before starting around the same corner.

Parker was waiting for me. "Look, Dodge. I told you all I'm going to say. You can't follow me around all day. That's harassment."

I tried to act casual, wondering if I could get arrested for harassment. "I'm just working on a story. This is my work."

"You're interfering with *my* work. I'll get a restraining order. No problem. Now cut it out."

A restraining order is civil, but I knew it might lead to other things. The circles between the DA's office and the police ran pretty small. I let Parker go for the time being, but I wondered why Parker would want to stop me from following him at that moment? I thought I would look around the neighborhood, just to make sure.

I had an appointment with Mike, my psychologist. Mike was actually a bartender, but people give you more respect when you say you are using your lunch hour to see your psychologist. For me, psychology is really a waste of money. Most of the time I just need to talk to someone with their head on straight while I knock back a gin and tonic.

Mike looked like an ex-navy type: a tough guy with big forearms, who wasn't afraid to fight. In reality, Mike had a degree from an Ivy League school, and he started his bar business with seed money from his trust fund.

"So you think Parker's the vigilante?" Mike asked. "What did you call him? The Midnight Watchman?"

"I'm just using that for now."

Mike was a friendly critic. "I like it. The Midnight Watchman!"

"Well, I gotta check with Legal, and see if it's trademarked," I said. "Do *you* think it could be Parker?"

"Why do you think he would *want* to be a super hero?"

"What are you talking about?" I said. "That's why people become cops in the first place."

"Yeah, but if you're right, then he's not giving himself credit for the arrest."

I nodded. He had a point there.

Mike continued: "I don't know if you're looking at this the right way. Have a lot of people seen this character... The Night Shifter?"

I shrugged. Inwardly, I thought that 'Night Shifter' was the dumbest one yet. Besides, I thought he said he liked 'the Midnight Watchman.'

Mike waved his hands. "Anyway, a lot of people have seen him, but only at night. That's curious."

"Not really. He only comes out at night," I said.

"Yes, but what do people usually do at night?"

I paused. "Sleep?"

"Yes," Mike said. "And dream. Have you ever heard

of Spiritus Mundi?"

"Just the Yeats poem," I said. I thought back to my high school English class. "A vast image out of Spiritus Mundi Troubles my sight... something something... A shape with lion body and the head of a man; A gaze blank and pitiless as the sun..."

Mike nodded. "Yes. I think of it as a sort of Universal Unconscious: People's desires are tapped into one source, and that causes them to see the same image."

"But this is a real person," I said.

"Who's to say what forces can be conjured up by the Universal Unconscious? There is a great desire for people to see Justice. Maybe this desire has manifested itself."

I began to wonder how smart I was to drink gin for my mental health.

I snapped my fingers. "Okay, Mike. It's time to come back from the 60's. Why not just say, 'It's an angel'?"

"Well that's not very scientific, is it?" he said.

"You pagan types think that you can say any crazy thing, but still imagine that you're being *scientific* just because you left God out of it."

"Hey, you keep coming back for my help. You don't have to come here you know. There are plenty of other bartenders out there who are willing to listen."

"Yeah, but I can walk home from here," I said.

Back at the office, Scott gave me a stern talking-to. "I got a complaint about you from Detective Parker. He claims that you are interfering with his work, and he threatened a lawsuit."

"You're the one who sent me on this story. I'm just following the facts."

"Parker says he doesn't know who this Midnight

Watchman is."

"Oh no? Check this out, chief." I laid out a stack of papers on his desk. "I've got nine arrest reports here. Six of them have a witness at the scene seeing someone on the roof. All nine were *handcuffed* to a pole when the police arrived." I laid the reports out, and pointed to the relevant box on each. "And all nine list the arresting officer as *Parker*."

Scott was quiet for a moment. "That's a big coincidence."

"It sure is. It's only logical that Parker knows who the Night Shifter is."

"Night Shifter? I don't know about that one. But how about this: Maybe Parker doesn't know the Midnight Watchman. Maybe it's the other way around. Maybe the Watchman knows who Parker is…"

I went to the local electronics store, and the salesmen put his two top models up on the counter. He pointed to the more expensive one. "This one will intercept all the calls within a 20 mile radius."

"What about that one?" I asked.

"That one will do the same thing," he said.

"Is any of this illegal? You know, to intercept police calls? Would that be harassment?"

"What am I, a lawyer? Look, you want a scanner, I'll sell you a scanner. You want my legal advice? Don't do anything illegal."

The salesman gave me a good deal, and he had a guy install the scanner in my car for free. That night I was parked up on a hill in Eagle Rock with a glossary of radio terms, following along with the calls as they came through. I even had some donuts and coffee, just to be authentic. After a couple of really boring hours, I heard this:

"Hillside. Over. That's a Wyoming plate: 305 Romeo Tango Delta."

From my vantage point, I could look down at the miniature police car on the freeway, and I knew we were hearing the same call.

"Car 20, please report to 200 North Brand. See Detective Parker about a possible 459."

I drove down the opposite side of the street, keeping low in the car. If possible, I wanted to see Detective Parker without him seeing me. There was already a swarm of police cars parked nearby, with their lights flashing. I had arrived in time to see the two perps, handcuffed to each other with their backs facing the street light pole. Detective Parker was discussing matters with the police at the scene.

I drove past the crime scene and headed down an alley. Then I circled around behind the building and parked. I couldn't see anyone behind the building, so I hopped up on top of a garbage can and used that to reach the fire escape, and up onto the roof.

I crouched low, and crept over to the street side of the building. The tiny pebbles on the roof made a loud crunching sound, and I wondered if they could hear it over the sound of the police radios down below.

The street was startlingly bright compared to the darkness of the roof. I watched the policemen scurrying about below me, and then glanced over to my left.

And that's when I saw him: He was a large, muscular man, dressed all in black. He rose up near the edge of the roof, gazing down intently at the police cars. I eased my cell phone out of my pocket and tried to snap a couple of pictures. That was when he noticed I was there. And then I saw how fast he was.

He hit high gear, and then leaped onto the next building. I tried to size up his path, and scampered back down to my car. I drove quickly down the alley, and turned down another alley. I parked between two buildings, and got out of the car and looked around.

Suddenly I heard footsteps, and overhead a black figure leaped across the span between the two buildings. I got back into my car and drove till I reached a dead end. I got out of my car again, and used the hood to get over the wall. There was a sidewalk on the other side and I jogged along keeping an eye out. The buildings were spaced further apart here, so I expected he would have to come down to the street. Amazingly, I caught sight of him one more time, and I tried to keep up on foot heading in the same direction, but I got too winded.

I was doubled over, with my hands on my knees trying to catch my breath. It was near dawn and I could faintly make out the writing on the signs of the local businesses. It all looked very familiar. There was a coffee shop on the corner, a car wash and book store. This was the exact same spot where I had confronted Parker just a few days before.

I spent the next couple of days talking to people in the neighborhood to see if anyone had seen the Midnight Watchman. Not surprisingly, there were many accounts of hearing footsteps in the early morning hours, and of a dark figure moving swiftly among the rooftops, without the aid of reindeer.

It was on the afternoon of the second day when I met Mrs. Simon. She was among the many people who had seen the masked figure, but had not reported it for fear of being thought a crazy person.

"Well if you are crazy, you've got a lot of company," I said. "I've seen him myself."

"You have? Oh, good. I was starting to wonder. My neighbor, Shirley thinks I'm going a little senile. Would you like to come in for some coffee?"

Mrs. Simon kept a clean home with no clutter. We exchanged our tales of the super hero over a pot of tea.

"I'm not sure what I can tell you that would be useful to you," Mrs. Simon said. "I saw him about three months ago."

"Three months?" That was the oldest sighting that I'd heard thus far. "You may have been the first one to see him." I opened up my notebook, clicked my pen, and took a bite from a cookie.

"Is that right? Let me see. I came home late one night from work. I usually don't work late, but I traded shifts with someone." Mrs. Simon was acting out the scene, there in her living room. She pointed up. "There was a man up on the roof. I was startled, and I guess he was too. And he just... took off running like a banshee. That's all, really."

I closed my notebook. "That seems to be the usual story."

"I'm sorry I can't be more helpful," she said.

"Everything is helpful at this point. Tell me, do you live alone here, Mrs. Simon?"

"No, my son Reggie lives here, but he's out just now."

She showed me down the short hallway to where Reggie's room was, and opened the door so that I could look in.

"Has he seen this masked character?" I asked.

Mrs. Simon brought her hand to her chin. "I don't think he has. He hasn't *told* me about it."

Inside Reggie's room there were posters of super heroes on the walls. He even had little figures of super heroes on his desk. In the corner was a single framed picture, but the light wasn't on and I couldn't make it out. I walked over to see who was in the picture. It was just then that Reggie came home.

Reggie was about 25. He was a handsome lad, favoring his mother. Reggie had braces on both of his legs, and got around with a pair of forearm crutches.

Mrs. Simon greeted her son. "Hello, Reggie. This is Mr. Dodge. He was asking about the masked crusader I told you about."

I turned around and saw Reggie as he came into his room. "Hello Reggie. This is quite a room you've got here."

I was reaching out to the framed picture, but Reggie moved quickly into the room and knocked the photo away with one of his crutches. The frame fell face down onto the hardwood floor, breaking the glass.

Reggie didn't try to hide his indignation. "I've told you before, Mother. I don't like people coming into my room when I'm gone."

"I'm sorry Reggie," she said. "It's my fault."

I tried to sound calm. "I'd like to talk to you about that masked crusader, if you've time."

I reached down for the frame, but Reggie stepped in front of me. "I'll get it," he said. And he did, setting the frame back onto the desk, facing away from me. "I'm sorry I can't talk now, Mr. Dodge. I just got back from work, and I'm very tired now. Perhaps some other time."

I went back to see Mike. He gave me a prescription for a stout with my gin.

"I wouldn't worry too much about Reggie," he said. "He just felt that you were intruding on his privacy."

"Yeah, I get that. I just felt sorry for the guy. He can't hardly walk."

"You don't need to feel sorry for the disabled. I think

they just want to be treated as equals, and that is their right. Reggie has his challenges, and from what you tell me he sounds very well adapted. He can drive and he has a job."

I nodded. "Yeah, he seemed well adjusted, except for the habit he had of knocking things onto the floor and breaking them."

"He is a little touchy about his stuff," Mike said. "Think about that: He'd rather break that portrait than have a stranger look at it. Did he have a lot of other pictures?"

"No, just posters on the wall. That was the only framed photo in the room."

Mike nodded his head and took a sip from his stout prescription. "Interesting. I'll guess that photo has a lot of personal feelings attached to it."

I went back to the Simon home the next day. Mrs. Simon met me at the door. "I'm sorry to bother you, Mrs. Simon. I was just wondering if Reggie was here, perhaps I could interview him."

"Reggie's not here right now. I wanted to apologize to you for the other day. Reggie doesn't usually act like that. I've never seen him get so angry. Something must have been upsetting him."

"Well I feel very bad about that myself, Mrs. Simon. That framed photo was damaged, and I wanted to make that right."

She shook her head. "Oh, that's not necessary."

"Please, Mrs. Simon, as a favor to me. Won't you allow me to take the photo and get the glass repaired?"

Mrs. Simon was a guileless creature. She could never spot a shameless, lying opportunist. Like me. She relented almost too easily. "Oh, I guess that would be alright, since you feel so strongly about it."

Mrs. Simon disappeared down the hall and returned with the frame. "You're very kind to do this, Mr. Dodge. If you like, there's a shop over on Hillhurst that does this sort of repair."

"That'll be fine." It was all I could do not to grab the frame out of her hands. She handed it to me, and I casually glanced down at the 8 x 10 photo. Beneath the broken glass was Detective Parker with his arm around a younger Reggie at a Special Olympics event."

"This photo is very special to Reggie," Mrs. Simon explained. "That's Detective Ron Parker. He's Reggie's 'Big Brother'. He has been for about ten years, since Reggie's father passed away."

Reggie was waiting by his van when I returned from the framing shop. The frame was in a paper bag, and I handed it over to Reggie.

"We have to talk," he said.

We went for a drive in Reggie's van. "I'm not sure what all you've figured out at this point."

"I've figured out that you and Parker know a lot about this Night Shifter fellow that you're not telling me."

Reggie wrinkled his nose. "Night Shifter. Is that what you're calling him?"

"Either that or the Midnight Watchman. All the really good ones are trademarked already, and they're not even real," I said.

"I like Night Shifter better," Reggie said. He paused for a while, and I took in the scenery as we headed into Laurel Canyon.

After a point, Reggie decided to make a brief confession. "Parker doesn't know anything. He gets a call from a voice he doesn't know. The men are handcuffed when he gets there."

"And how do you know all this?"

Reggie looked over at me. "You still haven't put it together?" He smiled, and turned forward as we wound along Mulholland Drive. "I've got the best cover there is."

"You? But you're...I mean you can't..." I couldn't say it.

"I can't even walk, so how can I climb roofs and chase down bad guys?"

"Well, yeah."

"I don't know, Mr. Dodge. It's the strangest thing. I've always been this way. My legs don't work, and I've learned to get around with crutches." Reggie shrugged his shoulders. "I always dreamed about becoming a super hero. Not for real, but you know, just imagining ... the way kids do. You've seen my room. After I got older it was just a hobby. I traded comic books, but I never read them anymore."

Reggie shot me a sheepish look, and then turned back to the road. "Okay, so then one night I had this weird dream. I was running on the rooftops. It was a very vivid dream. Then I woke up and thought nothing of it. A couple nights later, same thing. Then one night I showed up where some guys were planning some sort of a robbery. There I am, up on the roof, and they're talking about how their going to do the job."

Reggie paused again, and shook his head. "I don't know how it works. I was just there. So I followed them into this liquor store. And somehow I'm super strong and ... boom, boom, boom. Tough guy stuff."

"And you're seeing all this *in a dream*?" I asked.

"Yeah, it's like I'm another person. So when I capture these guys, I noticed I had a pair of cuffs on my hip. Detective Parker gave a set to me a long time ago when I was a kid. So I used those to hold the bad guys. I

63

know Detective Parker's cell number, so that's the one I dialed."

Reggie paused, and looked over at me. "You don't believe me."

"Oh, I believe you. It's just the craziest thing I ever heard. So do you have any super powers?"

"Not really," Reggie said, and he tried to make an inventory. "I'm very strong, and I can run super fast. And I guess I have really good balance not to fall off the roof."

"That's it, huh?"

"That's it," Reggie said. And he smiled. His smile soon disappeared. "So now what? Are you going to tell?"

I had the strong impression that Reggie wanted to remain anonymous. "Who would believe it?" I said.

"Yeah, I guess you're right," he said. "But I needed to tell someone. That was driving me crazy."

"So now I guess I'll be the reporter friend of the Night Shifter."

"Yeah. We can have reporter friends."

"Okay, Reggie. I'll write up the story and leave you out of it. Hell, I'll even leave Parker out of it, if you want. You might want to think about calling some other detective once in a while."

Reggie smiled again. "Okay, I'll think about it." He paused. "You know, you almost caught me the other night. You're pretty fast."

"Yeah, I am pretty fast," I admitted. "Maybe I've got a little super hero in me, too."

The End

5 THE FUME OF SIGHS

Love is a smoke raised with the fume of sighs;
Being purged, a fire sparkling in lovers' eyes;

It was the most awkward of times. In former days, the girl's father would have told the suitor that he must 'fish or cut bait'; but in these modern times, a clever bachelor who could brave the occasionally awkward discussion with his girlfriend, might extend his adolescent courtship well into his middle age.

Guy was still only 25, and presented himself as an intellectual: wore glasses, was lean and hungry, and thought too much. But definitely not dangerous. Guy had been dating Jean for over a year, and staring into the refrigerator for the past five minutes. Guy was having yet another dangerous and awkward discussion that just happened to be about marriage.

"I didn't say I didn't want to go to your sister's wedding," he said.

"No, but you groaned," Jean said from the other room.

Jean was 23, very pretty, and very low maintenance. She was sitting on the couch next to the pizza and the TV remote. Jean had spent most of her life being "one of the guys" and now slightly wished she knew more about being a girl. Jean was wondering why Guy found it necessary to look for things in the kitchen whenever she wanted to talk. Jean hated having to raise her voice to be heard in the other room, and she hated chasing Guy around like a badger.

Guy finally reappeared in the living room with beer and Parmesan cheese. Chayefsky's "Bachelor Party" was paused on the TV.

"I can't groan?" he said.

"Not about my sister's wedding. It's supposed to be a happy occasion; a *very* happy occasion. So there is no groaning." Jean didn't want to sound like a nag.

"It's just that, I don't know, people at weddings make it their business to ask everyone else when they are going to get married," Guy said.

"Oh, I see. You don't want to feel pressured," she said.

"It's not that, it's... well yeah it's that. People expect, that after you've been dating for a while... I just don't want to feel pressured."

"But I'm not pressuring you."

"Not directly, but your folks..."

"Oh, so I'm to blame for things my parents say."

"I didn't say you're to blame." Guy realized that he should have shut up several moments ago.

"When have I ever said anything?" Jean said.

"Well, it's not what you say, but the way you look at me sometimes."

"The way I *look* at you sometimes? I can't believe I'm having this conversation."

"I just don't want to feel pressured." Guy reiterated.

"I'm not pressuring you. You think about things too much."

"I know. I worry too much. Everything scares me."

Jean was normally very calm, but everyone has a breaking point. "I mean I realize I'm not your dream girl. Obviously the idea of marrying me would be frightening."

Jean's voice was starting to go into the upper registers. Guy had hurt her feelings.

"Oh Jean, I didn't say that. It's just kids getting hurt all the time, and bills for college."

Jean got up from the couch and was reaching for her purse. "Well I wouldn't want to trouble you with all the problems with our children that we haven't even had."

"You're leaving?"

"I've already seen this movie." Jean pressed the play button, and the movie continued as she let herself out of the apartment.

Guy found himself at a very crowded party in some strange apartment. The layout was typical of what you might find in the north-side of Chicago: brick, 4 story walk-up. Guy noticed that everyone was dressed in retro 1950's clothing. Guy looked down and saw that he was wearing 50's style clothing as well.

"This is interesting," he said. "I think I'm dreaming."

Guy squeezed through the other party goers and spied a beautiful lady in the living room, surrounded by numerous beaus. She looked very similar to Jean and was approximately the same age. Their eyes met.

"Hello stranger, where did you come from?" she said.

"Who me? I think I'm just dreaming," Guy said.

"I bet you say that to all the girls."

"No, really I don't. I worry too much."

"Aww. Why don't you come over here and tell me all about it?" The lady patted the seat next to her.

Guy motioned towards another fellow. "Don't I have to take a number, or something?"

One of the beaus took umbrage and started to stand up, but the girl grabbed his arm. "Oh, sit down Tony. You can't even take a little joke. I swear sometimes, you're just a big baby."

The lady stood up and took Guy by the arm. "Let's go out on the porch. I need to get some air."

The porch was also crowded with people, and offered a view of the alley and the El tracks.

"I really am dreaming you know," Guy said. "That's not just a line."

"And what are you in real life?" she asked.

"I'm just like this, but I think I live in the future."

The lady laughed and patted her hands. "Oh, wonderful. Do you have a space suit and live on the moon?"

"No, but I have a girlfriend."

"Well, at least you're honest. Does she get jealous easily?" She leaned in close to Guy when she said this, very nearly nibbling on his ear.

"Not normally, but she did tonight."

"Did she catch you cheating?"

"Nothing like that. She said I didn't want to marry her because she wasn't my dream girl."

"Oh? And who is your dream girl."

"I don't know. I guess you are. I mean, this is a dream and you're very pretty." Guy sized her up. "Yep, I guess you'd fit the bill."

"You're sweet. I'll tell you what to do about your girl. Let's make her jealous."

She planted a big kiss on Guy, leaving lipstick marks on his cheek. Guy started to wipe it off.

"Don't wipe it off. Leave it there. Trust me. This is the way to deal with bossy girls."

Guy woke up. It was early morning. He rushed to the

mirror and looked at his cheek. No lipstick.

"Just a dream," he said.

Guy met Jean at the coffee bar.

"So we finally got the bridesmaid dresses. I think they're hideous, but who cares, right? I mean, it's Suzie's wedding. It's not about me." Jean paused and took a sip of her chocolate.

"Right." Guy said. He was staring into his cappuccino.

"Where are you today? You're not even listening to anything I'm saying."

"You got the bridesmaid dresses back," Guy offered.

"What color are they?"

"Uh... I don't know. Did you already tell me that?"

"No, but you're supposed to ask."

There was an awkward pause. "Uh, what color..."

Jean cut him off. "Guy, tell me the truth. Are you seeing someone else?"

Guy was surprised and also felt slightly guilty. "What? No! I mean ... no."

"I'm sorry, I don't know why I said that. I guess this wedding is driving me a little nuts."

"Join the club... What color is it?" Guy asked.

"Well, Suzie got them to be the same color as my eyes."

Guy leaned in to look at Jean's eyes.

"You don't know what color my eyes are?"

"I was just checking. There's this girl I met who had the same..."

Jean set her mug down very sharply. "I knew it!" Jean said.

"It's not like that."

Jean stood up. "Save it, Guy. I'm late for work already." And she was gone.

Guy wondered if Jean was starting to form a bad habit.

Guy found himself back at the party. The lady was standing by the phonograph, and noticed him standing behind her.

"There you are! I've been looking for you." She grasped Guy by the chin and turned his face aside to examine his cheek. "You've wiped it off. Afraid she'd get jealous?"

"Oh, she's jealous all right. Thanks a lot."

"Oh, she's here?" She looked around the room.

"No. She's in real life. I'm just dreaming again."

"Oh, she's from the future too. Can she fly a rocket ship?"

"No, she arranges tours for sporting events," Guy said.

"Uh huh. Aren't you going to ask what I do?"

"What do you do?"

"I'm an actress. Didn't you see the show tonight?"

Guy shrugged.

The lady continued. "Well, my paying job is a legal secretary. Would you like me to spell subpoena?"

"Maybe later," Guy said.

The lady rubbed Guy's head. "Don't be sad, future man. Your girl will come around. Girls get jealous. We like to. It's our nature." She paused for a moment. "But she will make it very difficult first."

"How's that?"

"Well, she is probably going to give you the first degree."

The lady took the role of attorney doing a cross examination. "Tell me... What is your name?"

"Guy."

"Tell me, Guy, where were you on the night of July

23rd, 1957?"

"I was at a party."

"And where was this party?"

"I don't know. Where are we?"

Carolyn turned to her friend standing behind her.

"Monica, where are we?"

Monica said, "1726 West Roscoe."

"I was at a party with a charming girl at 1726 West Roscoe," Guy said.

"And what did you do after this alleged party with the incredibly beautiful girl?"

"I don't know. I guess I woke up and went to work?

The next morning Guy was stepping off the El in the loop, and making his way to work. The lady's words echoed back from the night before.

"And where do you work?" she asked him.

"At the Times downtown."

"Oh, a reporter? I thought you said you lived on the moon?"

"No, I sell ad space," Guy said.

"A likely story, Guy. A likely story. And tell me, Guy, if that's your real name, did you happen to catch Miss Carolyn Beaumont in her dazzling premiere at the Chicago Theatre?"

Guy was in his cubicle working at his computer.

"A dazzling premiere? I wonder..." he said.

Guy stood up from his desk and made his way to another cubicle, where his friend Francis was sitting.

"Hey, where do they keep the microfiche of the old copy from, say, the 50's?"

Francis looked up from his screen. "Down in the basement. Hey get me some coffee while you're at it."

"Right.

Guy was scrolling through a microfiche copy of an

old paper, and thinking about Carolyn's words from the night before.

"Tell me, Guy, where were you on the night of July 23rd, 1957?"

Guy flipped through to the theatre section, and then slowed down until he saw the large print font of the Reviews. "Aha!" Guy scanned along with his finger on the screen. Blah, blah, blah. Holy cow! 'Carolyn Beaumont was dazzling as Sorrel Bliss in a revival of Hay Fever at the Chicago theatre'... How did I dream *that* up? 'Miss Beaumont is new to the Chicago theatre scene, having worked previously...continued on page 36.'"

continued on page 36.

Guy meant to scroll down to the correct page, but moved the knob in the wrong direction.

"Woops. Wrong way." And then Guy stopped cold. There on the screen was a large photo of a burned out building. The headline read:

"23 PERISH IN DEADLY BLAZE!

Guy read the caption. "A fire swept through the building late Friday, and many were overcome by the smoke and unable to exit the building. The building, which was located at 1726 W. Roscoe... Holy cow!"

Now Guy was moving through the party with a purpose. He spotted Carolyn dancing with someone. Guy grabbed Carolyn by the arm.

"Look, we have to go. You're in danger!"

"What? Ease up, Guy. I'm dancing with Teddy now." Carolyn disengaged her arm. "Wait your turn like a good boy."

"You don't understand. There's going to be a fire!"

"I think someone's been drinking too much."

"No, I just read about it in the paper. I'm from the future!"

Carolyn closed one eye and shot a sidelong glance.

"Well why didn't you tell me about it before?"

"I just found out today," Guy said.

"Uh-huh."

"Look, I read about it in an old newspaper where I work. I'll prove it. You were in "Hay Fever" at the Chicago theatre."

"That doesn't prove anything." Carolyn gestured around the room. "Everyone here knows that."

Guy grabbed Carolyn's arm again, and started pulling her out of the room. "Look, I don't have time to argue. You'll thank me later."

"Ouch! Guy, stop it! You're hurting my arm!"

Tony stepped in and grabbed Guy. "Okay, pal. I've had enough of your baloney."

Carolyn tried to intervene. "Tony, it's alright. We're just playing around."

Tony wasn't listening. He twisted Guy's arm behind his back and pushed him out of the apartment.

"Just because Carolyn's nice to you doesn't give you the right," Tony said.

Guy wiggled his arm loose and tried pushing Tony back. "You don't get it. There's going to be a fire!"

"No, you don't get it," Tony said. "There's going to be a beating if you don't get out."

Guy tried to push his way past Tony. "I've got to warn her!"

"Okay, that's it buddy. You asked for it now." Tony wound back and slugged Guy in the nose. Guy tumbled backwards down the stairs.

The next morning, Guy looked into the mirror. There was no blood, and no bruises.

"Well I guess my dreams can't hurt me. There is nothing to be afraid of."

That night Guy and Jean were at 'The Cajun Crawdad', eating quietly.

"You're still mad at me?" Guy asked.

"I'm not mad," Jean said. "I don't know why you think I'm mad."

"Maybe it has something to do with the way you keep storming out on me."

"It's this wedding. It's got my nerves on edge."

They ate in silence for a moment.

"What?" Guy asked.

"What's wrong now?" Jean said.

"You suspect something," Guy said.

"I don't suspect anything. Maybe you feel guilty about something."

"I don't feel guilty about anything. You keep asking me if I'm seeing another woman, and I'm not."

"Oh, you're precious," Jean said. "Talk about protesting too much. I didn't say anything about another woman and you feel the need to deny it."

"Well you did the other day."

"I don't know why I said that."

They ate in silence for a moment.

"Look, I just want to clear the air. I keep having this dream ... about the same woman."

Jean slammed her fork down. "I knew it!"

"You knew I was having a dream?"

"Well, no. But I knew you acted guilty when I accused you. See? That's intuition. I've got intuition! What's the name of your dream girl, Guy?"

"She's not my... It's just a dream, okay? I'm worried about her, that's all."

Jean shook her head and made a low hissing sound.

Guy was out in the street in front of the apartment, which was now ablaze. There was a fire truck out in the street with two hoses going.

Guy rushed over to one of the firemen. "Is everyone out? I think there's still people in there! I was in that party!"

"We got some people out. We've still got one man in there," the fireman said. "Look Sir, you've got to get back. We're doing everything we can."

Guy moved back to a crowd of on-lookers in their bathrobes. The apartment was burning out of control.

The person standing next to Guy said, "I'd hate to be in there right now. Those poor people."

A lady said, "I wish there was something we could do."

Guy looked at the fire truck. There was a fireman's jacket hanging from one of the doors. Guy looked at his own jacket. Guy took off his jacket and laid it down on the truck. He picked up the fireman's jacket and put it on. Guy put on a fire helmet.

"You can't get hurt in your dream," Guy said, trying to convince himself.

Guy looked over the truck and found an axe. Guy lifted up the axe and started over to the building. He heard the fireman yelling behind him. "Hey you! What are you doing? Get back from there!"

Guy turned around and yelled back. "You don't understand. I'm from the future!"

Guy rushed into the building.

Inside was a dense wall of smoke. Spots of fire were raging everywhere. Guy bounded up the stairs. A fire scorched Guy's hand.

"Ouch! Don't worry. Your dreams can't hurt you. Your dreams can't hurt you."

Guy crouched down low, and jogged down the hall to the apartment.

"Hello? Carolyn? Anybody?"

Guy heard someone crying. He rushed down the hallway to a door and tried to open it. It wouldn't budge. Guy shouted out: "I'm going to smash down the door! Back away!"

Guy bashed the door open with his axe. Inside the room there were two bodies lying on the floor. One was unconscious. Guy stood her up, and laid her over his shoulder.

Guy reached down to help the other girl up. It was Carolyn.

"Don't worry. I've got you. We can get out on the other side of the building. There's a ladder crew on the street."

They stayed together and rushed over to where Guy had seen the fire truck. Guy smashed out a window and hailed the firemen below.

"Hey! Over here! I've got two more!"

The fire crew moved a ladder over to the window. Guy handed the unconscious woman over to the man on the ladder. Then Carolyn got onto the ladder. After Carolyn was on the ladder, she looked back to Guy.

"Aren't you coming?"

"No. I'm going to see if I can help the others."

The fireman on the ladder held out his hand. "You better get out now buddy. This place is almost gone."

"I'll be fine," Guy said. He turned and rushed back into the building. There was a horrible crash. The building was consumed in flames.

Guy was wearing his nicest suit. He knocked at Jean's door.

Jean opened the door and poked her head out. "I'll be ready in a second."

Jean was in a beautiful dress that matched the color of her eyes. Guy was thinking that Jean was a knockout.

"Wow! You look great!" Guy exclaimed.

"You think so? I didn't really like this dress, but bridesmaids can't be choosers."

"It's beggars can't be choosers." Guy said. "And always a bridesmaid, never a... never mind."

Inside the apartment, Jean was running around fussing with things and getting ready. Guy looked at some pictures and things that were on the counter near the kitchen.

"Who are these photos of? All your family?"

"Yeah. My mom wanted to see if we had any old photos of Suzie."

Guy worked his way through a pile of framed photos, scanning the faces in each one. At the bottom was a picture of Carolyn.

"Hey Jean, who's this photo of?"

Jean came out of the bathroom, and looked at the frame Guy was holding.

"Let me see. Oh, that's Grandma! Pretty hot, huh?

"Yeah, she's a Betty," Guy said.

Jean teased him. "Guy likes my grandma." She paused. "You know, some people say I favor her."

"You have the same color eyes," Guy said.

"I thought you didn't know what color my eyes were."

"Let's not start that again."

That afternoon at the wedding reception, Jean and Guy were making their way through the receiving line. Guy noticed an older lady standing alone.

"Oh Guy, there's my grandma," Jean said. "Come on, I want to introduce you."

The older Carolyn didn't hear them approach.

"Grandma, I wanted to introduce you to my boyfriend, Guy."

Carolyn stared intently at Guy. "Hello, Guy. I feel... have we met?"

"Guy saw a picture of you this morning and he thought you looked hot, Grandma," Jean said. "Grandma used to be an actress, Guy."

"Is that right?" Guy asked.

"Just mostly amateur things," Carolyn said.

"Any Noel Coward?" Guy asked.

"Why, yes. How did you know?" Carolyn looked intently at Guy, trying to remember something. "So what are your intentions toward my granddaughter, Guy?"

Guy shot a look to Jean: 'See what I mean?' Jean tried to put on an her innocent face.

"My intentions?" Guy asked.

"Do you love her?" Carolyn persisted.

Guy didn't hesitate. "Yes. I do. I love your granddaughter an awful lot."

"So what are your intentions?"

"Do I have to have intentions? Can't people just date anymore without having intentions?" Guy asked.

"You're frightened, aren't you?" Carolyn asked.

"Grandma's got you pegged, Guy." Jean said.

"Not as much as I used to be," Guy said.

Carolyn grabbed Guy's hand and held it in both of hers. "Not as much, eh? Let me ask you this: would you go through fire for my Jeanie?"

"Yes, I would," Guy said.

"I believe you," Carolyn said. She turned to Jean: "You hang on to this one, Jeanie. You won't find many men who are as courageous as your Guy."

Jean was surprised. "If you say so, Grandma."

Jean looked at Guy as they walked away.

"What?" Guy asked.

"It's just that ... Grandma never has anything nice to say about anyone's boyfriend."

"What do you mean?"

Jean pointed toward Rob, the groom. "See my sister's husband Rob? Grandma hates Rob. She says he talks like a girl."

Guy mumbled to himself. "He does talk like a girl."

Suzie the bride threw the bouquet, and all the girls scrambled for it. Rob and Suzie had their first dance. Jean surreptitiously paid her five year old cousin twenty dollars for the bouquet. Guy danced with Grandma Carolyn and Jean cut in.

Jean looked strangely at Guy: "Are you trying to pick up on my Grandma?" she asked.

That night, Guy dropped Jean off at her apartment.

"Look Jean, I know we haven't been getting along lately, but ..."

"That's okay, guy. I've been a real you-know-what, acting suspicious and what-not."

"But Jean, it's just that. I don't know... Here, I know how to do this properly..."

Guy grabbed Jean's hand in his and dropped down to one knee.

"Jean, I love you more than I can say. I would do anything for you. All those other worries... I'm not going to let my fears control me anymore, Jean. I want to marry you, and that's all there is to it."

Guy pulled a ring out of his pocket.

Jean wiped a tear from her eye, and her voice was in the upper register. "Guy, I can't believe it. Are you proposing? I mean... Is that my grandma's ring?"

"She gave it to me this evening," Guy said. "When I told her I wanted to marry you, she pulled it off her finger and she told me that she wanted you to have it."

Jean knelt down next to Guy and put on the ring.

"Oh Guy, I've wanted this for so long. Grandma is so cool." Jean put her arms around Guy and kissed him.

"I may not be your dream girl, and you may not believe this, but you're the man of my dreams," Jean said.

"Oh, I believe it," Guy said.

Jean kissed Guy again.

"You are so conceited," she said.

The End

6 SURFEIT WITH TOO MUCH

And yet for aught I see, they are as sick that surfeit with too much as they that starve with nothing.

Nick had built the entire basement studio with his own hands, including all of the wiring and the acoustic panels. Right now those hands were picking out a new song on the guitar while Nick sang into a microphone.

Nick's wife, Molly, watched his performance from the other side of the glass, where Nick had built an impressive sound board mixer. Nick's best friend, John Trotter, held a pair of drum sticks, nodded his head and swung the sticks around the board, improvising licks. John and Molly applauded wildly when Nick finished, which brought a smile to Nick's face.

Molly pushed a button that let her speak through the microphone, so that Nick could hear her in the studio. "That was awesome, honey. Best one yet."

John edged over next to Molly and spoke into the microphone. "That was great man. I could hear the drums already. This is going to be huge."

Nick shook his head. "You always say that."

John was adamant. "But this time I can *feel* it."

Molly interjected, "This could be a big hit, *unless* Roddy James has already written it."

Nick frowned. "Don't even joke about that. I don't even want to think about that."

John agreed. "Yeah, it's not even funny."

Molly was not dissuaded. "It should give you confidence. Think about it: You write songs that happen to sound like the best song writer in the world."

Nick came out of the studio and opened the door to the mixing room. "It's a small consolation when nobody wants to sign you. The last publisher I sent my songs to said I was going to get sued."

John chimed in. "And the owner of the Ace of Clubs said we should be a Roddy James tribute band. A *tribute band!*"

Molly put her fingers in her ears. "Yes, I've heard this already. You boys love to pout. You make me depressed when you go on so."

Nick gave Molly a hug. "I'm sorry, love. No more depressing talk. I'm going to be optimistic. Today is the first day on the sunny side of the street."

"It's always darkest before the cloud gets its silver lining," John added, nodding his head.

Molly smiled. "Fine. You can make fun of me, but I think your luck is going to change, Nick. I can *feel* it."

As if on cue, they heard the chime of the doorbell upstairs.

"Oh, I think that's the package I ordered." Molly said as she jumped out of her chair and dashed upstairs to get the door.

It was a small but comfortable home: walls were of unfinished wood, and the wood floor was covered with wool rugs. Nick had built and remodeled nearly all of it. Even the furniture had been designed and built by Nick.

Molly did not find the deliveryman at the door, but

instead there was a man dressed in a black suit, and wearing sunglasses. He handed Molly a card. "Hello. I'm a representative of Roddy James' music. I'm looking for Nick Swan."

Molly eyed the card suspiciously. "What's this about?"

The man smiled. "I'm sorry, but I've been instructed to speak only to Mr. Swan."

"Are you a lawyer?" Molly asked.

"No ma'am."

Nick came up from behind Molly, having heard the conversation. "Listen, I'll tell you the same thing I told the publisher: I never copied any of Mr. James' music. I wrote that song long before I heard the album. Besides, if he wants to sue me, he's not going to get anything anyway." Nick turned to look at Molly. "We're poor, aren't we honey?"

Molly kissed him. "That's right. We owe money to church mice."

The man in black regarded Nick. "Mr. Swan? I represent Roddy James music. Mr. James wishes to meet with you."

This caught Nick by surprise. "With me? When?"

"Today if possible." The man gestured at the limousine behind him.

"Roddy James wants to see me? The *rock star*, Roddy James?"

The man in black nodded. "That's the one."

Nick looked at Molly, confused. "Should I get a lawyer?"

A short time later, Nick was sitting in the back of the limousine, talking to the man in black, who was now driving. "I've always heard Roddy James was a mysterious guy. He never tours, never does interviews. He just makes albums." Nick paused, and looked around the limo. "*This* is pretty mysterious."

Nick examined the limo. He opened a refrigerator and took out a soda. "I'm going to help myself to one of these sodas, okay?"

"Feel free," said the man in black.

Nick sipped the soda and contemplated. "You always hear stories about Roddy James. You know the ones: how he supposedly sold his soul to the devil for the ability to write songs." Nick paused. "Did he?"

The driver looked back at Nick through the rear-view mirror. "Did he what?"

"Sell his soul to the devil?"

"I don't believe so," said the driver.

"Of course you wouldn't tell me if he did."

"Probably not," said the driver. "He's my boss."

Nick made his way through the Roddy James estate alone. He walked through a large, lush garden, following a white stone pathway, set in Irish Moss. After this, a hard, red dirt path ran along a high hedge. Nick entered through a pass in the hedge and found a large swimming pool surrounded by yet another beautiful garden.

Across the pool, Nick recognized the famous Roddy James. Roddy was smiling at Nick, as though they were old friends.

"And here we are," said Roddy James.

"Hello, Mr. James. It's a pleasure to meet you. I've heard all of your music."

Roddy James greeted Nick and shook his hand warmly. "My music. Did you like it, Nick?"

"I think you're a great songwriter. Maybe the best ever," Nick said humbly.

"I don't know about all that," Roddy said.

Roddy and Nick stood for a moment in silence.

Roddy spoke up. "I suppose you're wondering about all this."

"Well, yeah. It's kind of a surprise. Spur of the moment, you know. I had to cancel my lunch with Mick Jagger."

"Yes. Well, today is a special day. For you. Today is the first day of the rest of your life," Roddy said.

"That's funny, I was just saying something like that this morning to my wife. Of course, I was being sarcastic." Nick paused. "Did you ever think that there's some kind of ESP ...."

Roddy caught the gist of Nick's comment. "Between us, you mean? Do you think so?"

"Yeah. You must. You sent the car and everything. You're the famous one. I'm nobody."

"Oh, I wouldn't say you were nobody, Nick. I think you're incredible. I'm your biggest fan."

Nick looked confused.

Nick followed behind Roddy as he led them into the mansion. Down a hallway, Roddy opened an enormous wooden door, and turned on the light.

"You'll have to forgive me, Nick. I've made a little sort of a room for you here."

"A room? For me?" Nick looked around the room. Inside, it looked like a Nick Swan museum. On the wall were large photographs of Nick: one of Nick and Molly's wedding; another of Nick and John playing in a band.

"What is this? Are you playing some sort of a joke?" Nick asked.

"I told you, Nick. I'm your biggest fan. Look..." Roddy walked over to the corner of the room, where there was a large screen TV. Roddy pushed the control on the media player, and a video of Nick and John came on the screen. They were playing in a small club. Hidden speakers faithfully produced the sound of Nick's performance.

Nick looked at the screen, and then back to Roddy, who was beaming.

Roddy pointed to the screen. "That was at the Sacred Grounds Cafe. That was a great show."

Nick was confused. "You were at that show?"

Roddy nodded. "Incognito. I had a photographer shoot this with a camera disguised as a basket of fruit."

On the screen, Nick and John were smiling as they performed on the little stage. They appeared to be having a good time. Onscreen, Nick said, "I want to dedicate this next song to my wife, Molly." Onscreen the camera/basket of fruit did a clumsy pan over to Molly, who was smiling broadly, although her face was slightly flushed.

Roddy walked up to the screen and pointed to a figure in the background, wearing a beard and sunglasses. "That's me!" he said.

On the screen, Nick started playing another song. In real time, Nick watched his performance from several years before in stunned silence.

Later, Nick and Roddy sat in an enormous living room drinking coffee. The room looked similar to Nick's home, only larger and with nicer furniture.

Roddy said, "I guess it's time we got down to business." He slid a twenty page document across the table to Nick.

Nick picked it up. "What's this?"

"It's a contract. I had my lawyer draw it up."

Nick leafed through it. "I'm not a lawyer. What does it say?"

Roddy poured himself another cup of coffee. "Basically, I'm offering to buy your songs."

Nick was amazed. *"You're* offering to buy *my* songs? The most successful song writer in the world wants me to write songs for him? How many?"

"All of them," Roddy said.

Nick looked at the contract. "For how long?"

"For as long as you like." Roddy paused. "For the rest of your life if you like." Roddy looked at his watch.

Nick's hands started to feel a little sweaty. "How much for all this?"

"Look on page 6. About halfway down."

Nick turned the page. "That's a lot of money! Are you kidding? That much?"

"I thought you'd like that," Roddy said. "I'm giving you a lot more than any record company would. You'd even be making more than me."

Nick put the contract down. "I don't get this. What's going on? Why do you want to buy all my songs? The publishers don't want them."

"What are you afraid of, Nick? It's not like I'm trying to buy your soul."

Roddy smiled, but Nick was still distrustful.

Roddy looked at his watch again. "Oh, it's almost time. Look, are you interested in a swim?"

"I love to swim," Nick said.

Roddy smiled. "I know."

Roddy opened a glass door out to the deck, and gestured to the enormous swimming pool. "Keen pool, eh?"

"It's perfect," Nick said.

There was a small camera crew, video taping down by the pool. The director called out to Roddy: "We're ready anytime, Mr. James."

"Okay. With you in a sec," he called back.

Roddy led Nick over towards the pool house.

"What are they shooting?" Nick asked.

"It's a video," Roddy said. "You want to be in it?"

"Sure."

"I've got just the swim suit for you." Roddy opened up the door to the pool house and held out a hanger with some white silk pajamas.

Nick looked at the pajamas and back at Roddy. "A swim *suit*. Very funny. You're a strange man, Mr. James."

Later, Nick was feeling refreshed from his swim. He lay back in a reclining pool chair with a large, icy lemonade at his elbow.

Roddy settled into the chair next to Nick. "Let me tell you a story about a Rock Star."

Nick had seen a documentary of Roddy's life on television, but he was hoping to hear the *untold* story.

Roddy's voice took on the tone of one telling a fairy tale. "The Rock Star was born in a small town. Both parents were musical, and he learned piano and guitar at an early age."

"You too, eh?" Nick was amused at how many ways Roddy's life was like his own...

"Soon, he was playing in his own band. During high school, he played at dances and toured all the local clubs. He was good friends with a fellow on his football squad, and his friend became the drummer in his band."

Nick tried to remember who Roddy's drummer was...

"Around about that time he also met a girl, and they fell in love."

Nick was surprised by this version of Roddy's life. Very little of this had made it into the documentary.

"It wasn't long before they were married. And it was at this point that something significant happened to the Rock Star. Although he had always been able to play music, suddenly he found a great facility for *writing* music. And that began a very prolific period for the Rock Star. He was golden.

"He later said that songs would come to him suddenly. Sometimes in dreams; on walks; just about anytime.

"But what songs! The Rock Star just kept writing hit after hit. He was putting out more than one album a year, and every song would go to the top of the charts.

"Things went well for the Rock Star. He made a lot of money. He built himself a mansion with a swimming pool.

"And that's when things took a turn. Do you know what happens when you get everything you want?"

Nick scratched his head. "Uhm.... You run out of places to put your stuff?"

Roddy continued his story. "The Rock Star was going on tour, and ... let's just say it was not difficult to make new friends. And of course the wife caught wind of these affairs. And she wasn't too happy about it.

"But the Rock Star was weak. Women would literally throw themselves at him. Who was he to turn them away?

"And then there was the drugs. The Rock Star had been a straight arrow when he was younger; but when you're on the road you meet a lot of people, and the drugs were easy to come by.

"Soon the Rock Star was using drugs to give him energy for the shows. The drugs were a big strain on the band. They started quarrelling, and then they split.

"The Rock Star got a new band, but the problems just got worse. The Rock Star needed pills to wake up, and then pills to go to sleep. He needed pills to perform on stage...

"This was all very hard on the Rock Star's marriage.

His wife figured *'what's sauce for the goose...'*, and she started making friends of her own.

"Then his wife left him.

"So he drank more, and took more pills.

"I don't need to tell you where this is going. It's an old story. Boy meets girl. Boy becomes famous and cheats on girl. Boy gets a terrible drug problem. Boy loses girl...

"Everything must come to an end, and the Rock Star's songwriting was no exception. It left just as suddenly as it had come.

"It was surprising that it lasted as long as it did: In seven years, the Rock Star had written over two hundred songs that ended up in the top forty. He sold millions of albums, and had songs covered by singers of every stripe.

"But then, suddenly everything the Rock Star wrote sounded dull and uninspired.

"So he retired. But the Rock Star was not comfortable in retirement. He regretted the loss of his talent. He felt that the universe had spurned him, and he was angry.

"The Rock Star was soon locked in a cycle of despair and self-pity. He cut himself off from the outside world and quickly spiraled out of control.

"It was literally a race to the bottom, and the Rock Star lost. They found him in his swimming pool. It was ruled a "Death by Misadventure", but you have to wonder."

Roddy paused and sipped his drink. Nick stared thoughtfully at Roddy. Up until the rock star died, Nick had thought that Roddy was telling his own life story.

Roddy pulled out a faded yellow newspaper and read from it. "While many in this world perish from want, the Rock Starr suffered from a surfeit of riches. He had everything he could desire, except perhaps a means of controlling his own appetites. He had been graced with one of the greatest musical gifts ever bestowed on a mortal. And when that was taken away, he drowned in his own sorrow."

Roddy looked up at Nick.

Nick was surprised. "That's the end? That's kind of a bummer ending. Are you thinking of making a TV movie about this?"

"No, the story's not over yet," Roddy said. "Now comes the *weird* part."

"There was a Fan of the Rock Star. The Fan only met the Rock Star one time, and the Rock Star probably didn't even remember him. The Fan's room was filled with memorabilia: concert ticket stubs, photos and posters, and the prized autograph of the Rock Star.

"The Fan didn't have any real musical talent of his own. But he had every recording of the Rock star.

"When the Fan heard of the Rock Star's demise, it hit him very hard. It was like a betrayal. He felt that someone who had been given all that adulation, and praise, and love had no right to kill himself that way."

"I thought it was Death by Misadventure," Nick said.

Roddy shook his head. "The Fan didn't feel that way."

"It was on the third anniversary of the Rock Star's death that the young Fan had a life changing event. There was a memorial with hundreds of fans. Many hundreds of people were carrying photos of the Rock Star, and holding lit candles. They sang his old songs.

"The Fan brought his songbook to the rally and sang with everyone else, but beneath it all, there was still a sense of betrayal and resentment.

"Afterward, the Fan went to a bar and sat down to have a drink. As it would happen, the Fan met a man who claimed to be a top government scientist. The

Scientist said that he was in charge of a secret government project.

"After years of work, and billions of dollars spent on research, the program was being cancelled. So the Scientist was in the bar, getting hammered.

"The Scientist was eager to tell someone about this invention that was soon to be destroyed. The Fan was fascinated as he watched the Scientist make drawings on bar napkins, and used tumblers of whiskey, plastic straws and olive forks to explain the process. The Scientist was drunk, and the Fan didn't understand any of the technical language, but as far as he could make out: Time was really just a bunch of strings. By rotating some massive weights around a central chamber, the gravitational field that separated strings of time became weakened. At this point a laser could fuse different strings together. By fusing these strings of time, the Scientist could join a point in the present to a point in the past or future. He had invented a time machine.

"But just that morning, the Scientist had received notification that the program was being dismantled. The very next day, a team would be sent into the lab to take the time machine apart. The Scientist was completely bewildered by this insane action, but getting extremely drunk seemed like the best response.

"The Fan had difficulty believing the Scientist's story about a time machine, which would seem to be the normal reaction from someone hearing such a story. But the Scientist would not have it. His greatest achievement in life was going to be destroyed, and the only person he had told about it didn't even believe him. This, he could not bear.

"The Scientist grabbed his coat, bought a bottle of whisky, and the two of them headed off to the lab.

"The Scientist was too drunk, so the Fan drove. All

the way over, the Fan's mind was racing. Surely everyone has thought about the possibility of going back in time. But if you had one chance, where would you go? Or rather, when?

"Just outside the military base, the Scientist got behind the wheel, and the Fan ducked behind the seat. The guard at the station waved the Scientist through. They parked outside a remote building, and the Scientist let them both in. The Fan and the Scientist were alone in the lab.

"In the center of the room was a small glass chamber, and this was surrounded by a circle of several large metal cylinders. The Scientist showed the Fan how to work the controls, and how the time gauge worked. Then the Scientist placed the bottle of scotch and the Fan's songbook inside the glass chamber. He pushed a button on the console, and the giant cylinders began to rotate. Then the Scientist pulled a lever down, and the machine automatically maneuvered several lasers about.

"Soon those massive cylinders were moving so fast that they were a blur. The Scientist pointed to a blinking readout on the console and said that the gravitational field inside that rotation had become destabilized. The lasers automatically began fusing those strings of time according to the pre-set gauge on the console. Then there was a click, and the machine began to slow down. When the cylinders stopped rotating, the Fan could see clearly into the glass booth. The book and bottle were gone!

"The Scientist kept his eye on his watch, and casually walked over to the booth. He was quite tipsy at that point, but he managed to get to the booth just as the bottle and the songbook reappeared.

"The Scientist grabbed the bottle and held it aloft in celebration. 'Now do you believe me?' he asked.

"Who could doubt it? The Scientist continued to

drink and rant about the foolishness of dismantling this great achievement. But the Fan wasn't listening.

"The Fan was staring at the songbook that was still in the glass chamber. He could send the Rock Star's music back in time *before it was written.* If he sent the songs back far enough, he could pass himself off as the author.

"It wasn't long before the Scientist had drunk himself out cold. The Fan knew how to operate the time machine. He set the time gauge for two years before the first song was written. That would give him plenty of time to copyright the material and get it recorded.

"The Fan turned on the machine, and then ran into the glass booth as the huge cylinders began to rotate. He sat down in the glass case with the songbook on his lap. He took a big swallow of whiskey, and closed his eyes. The lasers moved into position and pointed at the case. And then everything went black.

Nick and Roddy were now seated in the projection room. Nick was incredulous. "You're telling me you went back in time?"

"Yep. But the story's not over yet." Roddy took a drink from his margarita.

"It sounded like it was over," Nick said.

"Nope. Now, imagine the man who wrote the songs."

"I thought you wrote the songs." Nick poured himself another margarita.

Roddy shook his head. "Nope. I *stole* them."

Roddy clicked on the remote, and the big screen TV showed a hotel ballroom scene of Nick and Molly getting married, and cutting the cake.

"Hey, that's me!" Nick said. "How did you get this?"

"You remember that the Rock Star had begun writing songs after he was married? If you went back in time and you knew the date two people met, and what date they got married, it would be very simple to get this footage. Wouldn't it?"

The TV cut to a park scene. It was shot from a distance, with a directional microphone picking up the sounds of a younger Nick playing a song for a younger Molly. When Nick was finished, Molly was smiling, but she was not overwhelmed.

Roddy was narrating the scenes on TV. "So the Rock star got married, but at this point, all of his songs were unoriginal. They had already been done."

The TV cut to another distant shot of a younger Nick, shot through his apartment window. Nick was writing in a notebook, and then stopping to play chords on his guitar.

In the present time, Nick watched the video and shook his head. "I can't believe this."

"Did you ever get the feeling you were followed?" Roddy asked.

On the screen, the younger Nick put his notebook away and turned off the light.

Roddy continued telling the story. "Whenever the Rock Star was inspired to write, it always came out like someone else's song."

On the TV, Nick and his band were playing, and the people were dancing.

Roddy provided the voice over: "So the Rock Star continued to play with his band, but he never hit it big. He just got older. He and his wife stayed in love, but they were never able to have children. He and his best mate never split up the band, but they stopped getting gigs."

The TV cut to another bar scene. It was a smaller crowd. Nick and his band were a little older. Nick was playing and singing, but his heart wasn't in it.

Roddy continued: "And whenever he heard Roddy

James on the Radio, he felt like..."

Nick cut in: "Like he was... Like I was listening to my own music."

Nick was suddenly feeling very sober, staring at Roddy, who smiled back at him. "Because *you were* listening to your own music," Roddy said.

"That's insane."

Roddy shook his head. "You said it yourself. You've always felt that I was writing your music. Because I *stole* it, Nick."

Roddy pulled out a song book. Nick was on the cover, dressed as a rock star. "This song book has every song you ever wrote."

Nick was amazed. He flipped through the book, and stared at the pages of music, which were interspersed with publicity photos. The pages had started to turn yellow. Next to the title of every song, it said that the music and lyrics were written by "Nick Swan".

Roddy sat back and drank his Margarita. "Careful with that. It's kind of old."

Nick saw that the song book had photos of Nick on his estate and in his swimming pool.

Roddy nodded towards the book. "That book has all the important dates of your life. It's got pictures of your estate." Roddy gestured around him. "I made this place based on those pictures. I never actually went to your house, but this is what it looked like."

Nick walked over to the window and held the book up, adjusting the angle. The view of the estate in the picture was a perfect match.

"You see?" Roddy said. "The pool is exactly what you see here. The Architects were working from these photos."

"But what about your life?" Nick asked.

"Yes. That's a good question. Well now, in *this* world,

there are two of me."

"You're kidding."

"Nope. I've seen him. People tell him he looks like me. I had to change my name, of course. And of course, I'm not missing yet, because the day I went back into the past is still in the future." Roddy paused, and took another drink. "Weird, huh?"

Nick sat down, confused. "When did I ... er. When did I ...."

"When did you die, Nick?"

"Yeah. I mean, am I going to ... die?"

Roddy smiled. "That's the best part. Let me show you."

Roddy clicked the remote again. "This is just a rough cut that the film crew made today."

The TV showed a picture of Nick that was taken from a newspaper clipping, where Nick was dressed in white silk and lying dead on the bottom of the pool.

"That's you. Or that *was* you," Roddy said. "Now watch."

On the TV, the newspaper clipping changed into a live action shot of Nick, wearing the identical silk suit in the footage shot earlier. Nick got up from the bottom of the pool, and swam to the surface of the water.

Nick was watching himself on the TV, paddling in the pool and taking instruction from the director, as he had done just hours before. "Like that? Did I do it right?"

"Yes. Perfect." the director said.

"This is going to be a video?" asked the Nick on TV.

Roddy shut off the video. "I don't think you're going to die," he said. "Not soon, anyway. Do you know what today is? This was the day they found you in your pool. Look."

Roddy held out the ancient newspaper clipping: It featured a photo of Nick, drowned at the bottom of the pool. "That's why we went for a swim at that hour. It was my own little ode to irony."

Nick was staring at the photo of himself, dead. "But my songs..."

"Yeah. They're your songs. You didn't get to write them in *this* world. But they're your songs, trust me. I didn't write them."

"But you want to buy them from me?" Nick asked.

"Yes. I want you to affirm what I did. You had everything, and then you ruined your marriage, and your friendship, and you killed yourself. What can you do for someone who has everything and makes himself miserable?"

"Take it all away," Nick said to himself.

Roddy nodded. "You can see I haven't suffered, Nick. But I want you to affirm what I have done. Was I only justifying my own selfishness?"

Nick didn't answer.

"I always wondered how you were going to take this." Roddy said.

"You stole all of my work." Nick said. "But if you didn't, I would be dead right now. You kind of saved my life."

Roddy shrugged. "I guess. The way I see it, you have a choice to make: You can take your life the way it is, or I can go back in time and take the book away from myself. I would be willing to do that."

Nick shook his head. "But then I would die. That would be stupid."

"You're taking this much better than I thought." Roddy said. "Of course, you've got three years to make up your mind. That's when I met the Scientist: In three years."

Nick flipped through the book. "So what do I do now?"

Roddy sat down next to Nick. "I don't know, Nick. I guess that's up to you. I've had a lot of time to think about this." Roddy gestured around. "You see all this? It really belongs to you. You can have it."

"You're giving it to me?" Nick asked.

"Why not? This whole place was bought with *your* songs."

Nick shook his head. "I gotta think about this." He looked down at the songbook he was still holding. "Can I keep this?"

"Of course. It's every song you ever wrote ... or didn't write."

Nick nodded and absently flipped through the pages. Suddenly, a thought struck him, and Nick started thumbing through the book, looking for something. "Every song?" he asked.

"That's right. That's over two hundred top 40 hits."

Nick was smiling as he went through the book. "It's not here," he said. "The song's not here!"

"Of course it's there," Roddy said, dismissing the idea. "That's a compilation of your entire catalogue. It was published after you died."

"It doesn't have the song I wrote this morning. I wrote a song this morning, and my wife said it was the best one I've ever written."

Roddy looked up. "A new song? That's amazing! Do you realize what that means?"

Nick shook his head. "Maybe. I don't know."

"You *really are alive*, Nick. I didn't just save your life, I saved your creativity. Nick Swan, the greatest songwriter who ever lived, isn't finished yet! This is the beginning of something big. I can feel it!"

Nick got another idea. "Hey Roddy, can I borrow your car?"

"Sure, buddy. George will take you anywhere."

Nick was already running toward the car. "Thanks."

Roddy shouted after him. "Any time. You know where to find me. You've got three years!"

Nick walked in through his own front door. He had only been gone for a few hours, but his life seemed to have changed entirely. Nick spied his wife in the kitchen and he smiled at her, holding up the song book. "Molly! You're never going to believe what happened!"

Molly smiled back at him. Nick couldn't see what she was holding in her hand. "Hello, Daddy," she said.

"You're never going to believe the story that guy told me," Nick said.

"I bet I've got a better story," Molly said.

"How could you have a better story? This is big! This is the most amazing story you've ever heard," Nick said waving the songbook.

"I'm pregnant," Molly said.

Nick was stunned. He hugged Molly. He was ecstatic. "Oh, baby. Are you sure?"

Molly held up the plastic pregnancy test sick. "If this sucker is right, I'm in a family way. Okay, what's your story?"

Nick laughed. He set the songbook face-down on the counter. "You're right. Your story's better. Your story's much better."

The End.

7 GLORIOUS TO THIS NIGHT

"O, speak again, bright angel! for thou art
As glorious to this night, being o'er my head
As is a winged messenger of heaven"

Life often finds us in unexpected and curious pairings of extreme differences: fortunate and unfortunate; rich and poor. One such example of this was in Boston, just after the second world war, in the Michaels' home on Commonwealth Avenue. It is not so much a home as mansion, but Lydia lived there.

The mansion was from the Victorian era, but it was well kept up. The walls were filled with many elegant paintings, and there seemed to be no end of large, well furnished rooms.

Rose was 24, beautiful, fresh from Ireland, with long, red hair. Rose had several duties in the Michaels' home, including cooking and cleaning. And most everything Rose did involved singing as well.

Rose's most important job was to care for Lydia Michaels, who was also 24, but could not care for herself. Lydia was blind and dumb, and had always been so. Lydia could not control her own limbs, but she could chew and swallow. And Lydia could smile.

Presently Rose was singing while she brushed Lydia's hair, and put it in a bow.

"You have such beautiful hair Lydia, but it's getting so long."

Lydia's mother was walking past and was drawn by Rose's voice. Rose saw Mrs. Michaels outside Lydia's room. "Hello, Mrs. Michaels."

Mrs. Michaels still spoke with a heavy brogue. "You're such a blessing to us, Rose."

"Oh, go on. I look forward to doing Lydia's hair. It's like touching silk."

"It looks beautiful, Rose. Thank you. Tell me, have you heard anything from your mother back home?"

Rose glanced toward Lydia before answering. "No ma'am. I haven't yet, but I'm sure they will write soon. You know how the mails are."

"I'm sure you're right. You'll likely be getting a letter today."

"Thank you, ma'am."

The radio had been playing quietly in the background, and when Rose heard the intro to the Django Reinhardt and Stephane Grappelli hit "After You've Gone", she rushed over to turn up the volume.

"Lydia, it's Django!" Rose said. Rose sang along with the radio:

"After you've gone and left me crying
After you've gone there's no denying,
You'll feel blue, you'll feel sad,
You'll miss the bestest pal you've ever had ..."

Lydia would make her particular smile when she heard this song.

"It's her favorite song," Rose explained

Mrs. Michaels was smiling as well. "I can see that."

Later, when Rose was coming home to her own apartment, she met Mrs. Neely in the hallway. Mrs. Neely was holding out an envelope.

"I think this is your letter, Rose. It must have gotten mixed in with ours and I didn't notice it."

"Oh thanks, Mrs. Neely." Rose paused as she glanced down at the backside of the envelope. "It's been opened!"

"Sam said it was already opened when he found it. I've already talked to him about other people's mail."

Rose didn't want to make a fuss. "I'm sure it's all right. Oh, it's from back home. I've been waiting for this. Thank you Mrs. Neely."

Rose excitedly opened the envelope and began reading the letter from her mother as she let herself into her apartment.

Later that evening, Rose was having dinner with her beau, Frank, who was 32, a handsome Irish-American. Frank liked to watch Rose when she ate. She managed to move her fork around a great deal, but never ate more than half of her food.

"Oh, I almost forgot. I got a letter from my mother finally. That Sam Neely fellow seems to have accidentally taken my mail with his own."

"That one's a delinquent." Frank said.

"Well then, we'll just have to pray for him."

"I don't know if that'll do any good."

Rose didn't like it when Frank talked that way. "It's funny you should say that."

"Oh, your letter from home is the result of a novena?" Frank asked.

"You know I'd never say a novena for something selfish, Frank."

"Well, what then?"

"Oh, you'll just laugh. I know you." Frank watched Rose's fork move around the salad. He thought he saw her eat something.

"Come on, Rose. You know you want to tell me."

Rose went through her purse and found a little notebook. "All right. But mind you: this isn't my own fancy, I've got *proof*. I've got *evidence*. I know you." Frank liked the way Rose said "evidence".

Rose leaned in closer to Frank, so as to avoid being overheard. "Well you know that girl, Lydia, that I care for?"

"The poor paralyzed girl."

"That's right. Well I noticed something about her. I think... Well, let me show you." Rose looked at her notebook as she talked. "You know, even though she cannot speak or see, she can hear."

"How do you know she can hear?"

"Because she *smiles*, Frank. Well, you know I *talk* to Lydia when I'm feeding her, or doing her hair. Oh, here it is: On March 17, I was changing Lydia's clothes and I happened to mention Mr. Parsons was sick after his heart attack. The *very next day*, Mr. Parsons went back to work, and he hasn't been sick a day since."

Frank nodded. Rose looked into her notebook.

"On April 6, I was feeding Lydia her dinner and I was talking about Mrs. Flaherty's husband losing his job, and how he has six children to support. The *very next day,* Mr. Flaherty found a job, and with more pay at that."

Frank nodded. "Okay."

Rose looked into her notebook. "Ah, here. Mrs. O'Toole's son Joe was hit by a car, and they thought he was going to die. I told Lydia April 23, and Joe lived! Not only that, but he came out of a coma and now he's back in school!"

Rose closed her book and smiled proudly. "And now, today, Mrs. Michaels mentioned in front of Lydia that I was waiting on a letter from my mother, and I got this on the way home from work. The *very same day,* Frank!" Rose held out the letter from her mother.

"So what are you saying?" Frank asked.

"I think she's an angel. Lydia. I think she's some sort of a saint or an angel."

Frank laughed. "Because of that?"

Rose waved her book. "I documented it."

"That could be coincidence. Post hoc ergo propter hoc. Just because it follows, that doesn't prove causation."

"Oh, I knew you would say something like that. You don't believe anything."

"But it's just so fantastic, Rose. You can't expect me to believe..."

"Why not? We believe that Saints can pray for miracles. Why not Lydia? She might be a saint. Why not? Hasn't she suffered her whole life? Not being able to move her limbs. But she can hear, Frank. When I told her about Mrs. O'Toole's son, she started crying. Honestly, Frank, tears were streaming down her cheeks."

"Fine, then. She's an angel."

"Oh, you're just saying that, but you don't believe it. That's what's wrong with you Frank. You have no faith."

"I can't help it, Rose. I'm a cynic. Now, if we had some real proof..."

Later Frank was walking Rose back to her apartment.

"Nothing would prove it to you," Rose said.

"We could make a scientific proof," Frank offered.

"Like what?"

Frank thought for a moment. "A test case. We will take something that has been needing help for a long time, with no change. Then you tell Lydia about it, and then we will see if there is a change. And it has to be soon afterward. Let's say two days."

"Oh, but you can't use her for something selfish, Frank."

"No. We'll take a true charity case. But it has to be a longstanding problem. And it has to be impossible."

Just then, a voice behind them called, "Mr. Flanagan."

Frank recognized the voice and winced. He turned around to see Miss Heath, who looked to be about 50, tall and thin, with beady eyes.

"Miss Heath. It's so nice to see you." Frank lied.

"I haven't got your rent check yet, Mr. Flanagan."

"I don't know why that is, Miss Heath. I sent it to you last week."

"Is that right?"

"That's right, and I don't like your insinuation," Frank said. "If you publicly impugn my character I might decide to sue you for slander."

Miss Heath changed her attitude. "Oh ... well I probably didn't see your check. I'm sure I missed it." Miss Heath turned abruptly and left without saying good-bye.

Frank watched her leave. "The old shrew."

"Is she your landlady, Frank?"

"She owns the building where I keep my office. I've never once been late with a payment. Ever. She's just trying to yank my chain."

Rose let out a slight 'tsk'. "Poor old thing's got nothing better to do. Is she a widow?"

"She's never been married, and it's no wonder. Who'd have that harpy?"

"She's probably lonely, Frank."

"Lonely with her millions."

"Poor old thing," Rose said.

"She's past praying for."

Rose's eyes lit up. "How about her then?"

"What?"

"What if we use your Miss Heath as an experiment?" Rose asked.

"You mean tell Lydia about lonely Miss Heath?"

"You said she's past praying for," Rose said.

Frank shrugged his shoulders. "Okay. Miss Heath. You tell Lydia about Miss Heath."

They got to Rose's stoop, and she gave Frank a goodnight peck on the cheek before starting up the steps. "I'll try, but I'm not promising anything."

The next day Rose was feeding Lydia some stew as she talked about Miss Heath.

"And she's just unhappy I think. I think if she had a boyfriend, maybe she wouldn't be so lonely. Don't you think so, Lydia?"

Lydia chewed her food, and for the thousandth time Rose wondered if there was any expression in her eyes.

A couple nights later, Frank and Rose were walking together, and they heard Miss Heath call from behind them. "Mr. Flanagan!"

Frank and Rose turned around to see Miss Heath walking arm in arm with a distinguished looking man. The gentleman was the same age as Miss Heath, and he had a large, gray mustache.

Frank sounded surprised. "Miss Heath?"

Miss Heath was beaming. "Well funny meeting you here. Oh, I guess I should introduce my friend, Mr. Carlyle."

"Nice to meet you Mr. Carlyle," Frank said, shaking his hand. "This is my friend, Rose McNamara."

They made small talk for a while. Mr. Carlyle seemed

to be very pleasant, but shy.

Miss Heath looked at her watch. "Well, I guess we'll be going now. We have tickets for a show, and we mustn't be late."

Mr. Carlyle nodded. "Yes, we must be going. Pleasure meeting you, both."

Miss Heath smiled proudly as they left. Frank stared after her for a moment. Rose walked on and Frank caught up.

"Did you tell your friend...?" Frank asked.

Rose had the expression of one who prefers the catbird seat. "Lydia? You know I did Frank."

"But... that's amazing. That old gentleman. I don't believe it."

Rose repeated what her mother often said: "There are more things wrought by prayer than this world dreams of."

"It's just so... I don't believe it."

"For those who believe, no explanation is necessary; for those who do not believe, no explanation will suffice."

"You're a regular Bartlett's quotations this evening," Frank said.

"I told you Frank: my Lydia is an angel."

"An angel? I don't know, but there's something here. Maybe she's some sort of mystic. Do you think she can see the future?"

"How would she tell you about the future Frank? The poor girl's mute. She's *paralyzed*. She can't move her limbs."

"I was just wondering. Perhaps, if we knew about future events, we could make preparations. Like for instance, if there was going to be another war, or the stock market was going to crash."

Rose did not take that well. "The stock market? Did I

hear you right?"

"It was just an example," Frank said.

"You should be ashamed of yourself, Frank. You witness a miracle, and the next minute all you can think about is your own selfish profit."

"I'm sorry, Rose. I've just got a practical nature."

"*Practical nature*! I'm tired of it Frank. I can't bear it."

Rose took off her ring.

"Now, take it easy Rosie."

"No, Frank. That is the limit. Take your ring back. I don't want it."

"Oh, Rose, calm down girl."

"No I won't. I've caught you reading the paper in church, and sniggering under your breath. And I've seen you *make eyes* when I talk about the Saints, but this does it. *You're* the one who's past praying for, Frank Flanagan. I know you and your practical nature. You're all about the bottom line."

"What's wrong with being practical?"

"Nothing. But some things are more valuable than money. Like people... and God and His Angels."

Rose handed Frank the ring.

"You can take your ring back to the jeweler. Maybe you can get a good deal for it." Frank was speechless as Rose hurried away.

The next day Rose was doing Lydia's hair. Rose's eyes were still damp from crying.

"I'm sorry I'm so gloomy, my dear. I had a little spat with my beau, Frank. It's just that... I shouldn't go on, but sometimes I wonder if he's the right one for me. He's handsome, and he's a good provider. But I want a man that's more like the ones back home. Men with faith. An old fashioned man. A knight in shining armor, like the ones in the storybooks. Am I being too selfish? I always thought, that I'd meet someone more heroic."

Later that evening, Rose was walking back home, her head down, not paying attention. She stepped off the curb, and a hand grabbed hers...

"Pardon me ma'am."

The hand pulled Rose back onto the sidewalk just in time to avoid a bus coming down the street.

The bus horn sounded loudly as it passed.

Rose looked up to see who had grabbed her hand, and found herself looking into the eyes of a man who reminded Rose of Tyrone Power.

"I'm sorry to have done that ma'am. The bus was coming, and I didn't think you saw." Lawrence had an Irish brogue.

"Oh, you saved my life. Thank you, Mr...."

"McFee. Lawrence McFee. It's a pleasure to make your acquaintance."

"Rose McNamara. You're from back home?"

"Cork. You?"

"Irish from Liverpoole."

Lawrence smiled. "Yes. Well, today is my lucky day. I was just hoping to save a beautiful Irish girl, and luckily you stepped in front of that bus."

Rose gave a little curtsy. "It was the least I could do."

"Listen, Rose. Have you eaten yet?"

"No."

"Neither have I. Would you like to have dinner?"

"I suppose," Rose said.

"When I grabbed your hand just now, I noticed that there wasn't a ring on it."

Rose felt her hand, forgetting for a moment that she had given back the ring. "No. I'm... single alright."

"Then you'll have dinner with me?"

Rose made up her mind. "I will," she said.

"That's grand."

Lawrence held his arm out for Rose, and the two of them set off to a nearby bistro.

The next couple of weeks flew by. Rose found herself making a checklist, and comparing Lawrence to Frank. Both men could make her laugh, although Lawrence seemed to be a generally happier person.

Lawrence would also do the little things without having to be told. Like getting flowers for no reason. And when they were in Church, Rose noticed that Lawrence would pray, whereas Frank seemed often to glance around the church.

Rose was smiling as she let herself into the Michaels' home.

Mrs. Michaels met Rose at the door and embraced her. Mrs. Michaels was crying.

"Oh, Rose. My baby..."

"Mrs. Michaels. What's the matter?"

"It's Lydia," Mrs. Michaels said. "It happened during the night."

"Is she all right?"

Mrs. Michaels shook her head. "She's passed on, Rose. Lydia's dead."

Rose was shocked. "No! She was fine yesterday."

Mrs. Michaels led Rose over to Lydia's room, where Lydia lay on her bed. She was not breathing.

The two ladies regarded Lydia sadly. "The doctor said it was an aneurism," Mrs. Michaels said. "She passed away in her sleep. Poor child."

Rose quietly made a prayer for eternal rest. "... *requiescant in pace. Amen.*"

"D'ya know, Rose. Lydia didn't have many friends in her life. You were her best friend."

Rose was still thinking about what Mrs. Michaels had said as she and Lawrence walked together.

"Rose? Did you hear me?"

Rose looked up. "What? I'm sorry. Were you talking?"

"You seem distracted." Lawrence said.

"Yes. A girl I knew... she died today."

"Oh, I'm so sorry. You must feel terrible."

"Yes. She was a sweet girl. She was an invalid all her life. I was just thinking about what her mother had said. I didn't mean to ignore you. What were you saying?"

Lawrence seemed suddenly bashful. "Oh, I feel bad saying this now... I'm leaving, Rose."

"You're *leaving*? Why?"

"Back to Ireland," Lawrence said. "My business here is finished. I told you it was only temporary."

"But it's over so fast."

"Yes. And I was saying, *I don't want to leave you*, Rose."

"And I don't want you to leave," Rose said.

Lawrence stopped, and held Rose's hand. "I don't have to leave you, Rose. You can come with me."

"Come with you?"

"As my wife. Please say you will."

"Oh, Lawrence. Everything's happening all at once. Lydia just died today, and now you're asking me...."

"I know it's sudden, dear, but I'm working with a deadline."

Rose reached up and grasped Lawrence gently by the chin. "I like you, Lawrence. You're a good man. You're handsome and you're kind. But..."

"But you don't love me?"

Rose shook her head. "I don't know. Am I expecting too much? Am I being selfish? I don't know if I should be expecting anything more. What more is there?"

Lawrence gazed into her eyes, waiting on Rose's answer...

Rose was deep in thought as she walked down the hallway towards her apartment.

Mrs. Neely was waiting in front of her door. She was wringing her hands. "Rosie, I've been looking all over."

"What's wrong?"

"It's my son, Sam."

"Is he all right?"

Mrs. Neely looked down, ashamed. "He's been arrested for robbery."

"I'm sorry," Rose said.

"That was two weeks ago, Rose. He's got a preliminary hearing tomorrow. I just got back from visiting him at the jail. My son says.... He says the public defender wants him to plead guilty."

"But he doesn't have to." Rose said.

"No, but the lawyer's got him all confused."

Rose shrugged her shoulders. "Well, sometimes they make deals. You know, leniency deals."

"But my boy is innocent."

"Well I'm sure he is." Rose said, half-believing it.

"He really is Rose. The night he was supposed to be... doing this crime... He was with me. He had dinner at my apartment."

"Did you tell this to the lawyer?"

Mrs. Neely was adamant. "Yes! And the police."

"Then why does he want to plead guilty?"

"My son's lawyer says that I'm not a reliable witness because I'm his mother. He says that any mother would lie for her child. But I'm not lying. I know I'm telling the truth."

Rose unlocked her door. "Here, Mrs. Neely. Come inside, and I'll make us some tea."

Rose crossed over to her phone and dialed. She turned back to Mrs. Neely. "I have a friend who knows about these things."

Rose listened to the phone. "Come on Frank. Pick up." She turned back to Mrs. Neely again. "He's not answering."

Rose hung up and walked back to Mrs. Neely to comfort her. "Look here: tomorrow I'll go down to the court with you, all right? Maybe we can talk to the judge."

"All right," Mrs. Neely said.

Rose went in to her kitchen and put the kettle on.

The next morning, Rose and Mrs. Neely sat in the back of the courtroom. Mrs. Neely was weeping and Rose was rubbing her shoulder. "Don't worry, Mrs. Neely. It'll work out. You'll see."

The bailiff told them all to rise, and that the honorable Justice Hollander would be presiding. Then the judge came in and sat down, and asked everyone else to sit.

The judge looked at the docket. "Okay, who's first?"

The court clerk said, "People v Neely."

Rose looked to Mrs. Neely. "Sam's next."

The judge looked out towards the holding cell that was to the right of the court. "Is Mr. Neely here?"

Sam Neely stood up. He was 19, with red hair that didn't seem to be on good terms with a comb. Sam wore a jail uniform and chains. He looked scared.

Sam's lawyer stood next to him, but Rose couldn't see the lawyer's face. Then Rose heard Frank speaking. "He is, your honor. Frank Flanagan representing the defendant."

Rose's head spun around.

The Judge looked pleased to see Frank. "Mr.

Flanagan. It's been a while since you've graced my courtroom."

"It's been too long, your honor," Frank said.

The Judge held up a motion. "Mr. Neely, I see that you've entered a motion for a change of plea?"

Neely looked to Frank, who nodded. Neely cleared his throat. "I'm sorry, your honor. I wish my plea to remain not guilty, your honor."

"Very well. Is the prosecution ready for the preliminary?"

The prosecutor stood up. "Your honor, we are not prepared. We thought there was going to be a change of plea."

The judge nodded. "Very well, we'll postpone that to another date. Is there anything else?"

"Yes, your honor," Frank said. "I've only been representing Mr. Neely for a short time, but as the court knows, Mr. Neely has no criminal record. He has never been arrested. We are requesting bail."

The prosecutor stood up again. "This is for robbery, your honor."

The judge shook his head. "He has no record. I don't see why he shouldn't have bail if he can post a bond."

"Thank you your honor." Frank turned to talk to Sam quietly, and the judge said something else that Rose couldn't hear.

Mrs. Neely started crying again. "Thank God!" She said.

Neely smiled at his mother before the bailiff escorted him back into the holding cell.

Frank put his files back into his briefcase and started to walk out of the court. Rose intercepted him. "Can I talk to you, Frank?"

"If you don't mind walking with me. I have to get

over to the bail bondsman." They walked down the hallway together.

"I was really proud of you today, Frank." Rose said.

"What did I do? He's not off yet, you know. We just got bail."

"I know. It's just that he was going to plead guilty, and now at least he has a chance. I tried to call you last night. How did you find out about the case? How is he paying you?"

"Sorry, doll. I can't talk about it. You know: lawyer/client relations. That's privileged."

"I understand… Look Frank, I… wanted to say I was sorry. I underestimated you."

"I don't think so, Rose. You got it right. I don't have a lot of faith. I guess I just don't trust people. Maybe I'm too cynical." Frank opened the door out of the court building and held it open for Rose.

Frank headed east at a rapid pace and Rose felt like she was almost jogging to keep up. "But today you… There's more to faith than just believing things. Faith means you have to do things too…"

Rose paused because she didn't know exactly what she meant to say. She changed the subject. "I have to tell you, Frank. After we broke up, I started seeing someone."

"I know all about that," Frank said. "I've seen you two around. He's quite the charmer, I guess."

"But that's just it, Frank. He had everything I wanted… everything I thought I wanted. But then when he proposed…"

Frank turned towards Rose in surprise. "Well, he's a fast worker. He already proposed? I imagine he must be late for a train."

"But I turned him down, Frank."

Frank stopped walking for a second, and Rose ran

past him. A broad smile came over Frank's face, and then quickly faded away. Frank started walking again. "See, it pays to be patient," he said.

"It wasn't that, Frank. I told Lydia I wanted a knight in shining armor."

"Oh? And your Angel sent you that fella?"

"Yes, and I thought he was the one. But then he proposed, and I realized I didn't love him."

"But if you asked an angel for something, don't you have to take what you get? I mean, if you turn him down aren't you being unfaithful?"

"Is that the way it works, Frank?"

Frank stopped again.

"I don't know how it works with angels," Frank said. "I don't know if I even... I try to be good, but I know I don't always succeed. But when we were together... when we were going out, it was like... you were *my* angel. I always tried to be good... for you. And I always felt that you gave me a little bit of luck." Frank paused for a moment, and then started walking again.

"And if that didn't work out, I can accept that," Frank said. "I can move on. But at least *I know* what I want. I'm not shifting back and forth."

"But I *do* know what I want Frank. That's what *I'm trying to tell you*. When I saw you today, and you saved that boy from jail. It was like you were a knight."

Frank stopped and looked at Rose.

They were standing in front of a street café, just next to the bail bondsman. The Quintette du Hot Club de France could be heard coming out from a radio in the café.

Rose looked deeply into Frank's eyes. "Like you were *my* knight," she said.

"Do you mean it Rosie?"

Rose nodded. "Yes." Then Rose heard the music.

"Oh listen Frank! It's "After You've Gone". That was Lydia's favorite song. It's Django Reinhardt! Oh, I love this song. Dance with me, Frank."

"What? Here?"

Rose grabbed Frank and they began to foxtrot together on the sidewalk in front of the café.

"There'll come a time, now don't forget it, baby
There'll come a time, when you'll regret it
Someday, when you've grown lonely
Your heart will break like mine
You'll want me only.
After you've gone."

The End

8 TIME IS BROKE

How sour sweet music is,
When time is broke and no proportion kept!

As fate would have it, a bearing in the centrifuge broke down. Luckily, had spare on hand. Half-hour later everything was ready. At last, the moment of triumph had arrived!

Placed that morning's copy of the Times inside the Chamber. Set time for plus 10 minutes.

New tube worked perfectly, and gravitational flow quickly reached 100%. Newspaper motionless. Then visual pattern interrupted at regular intervals. After one minute, both table and newspaper disappear.

Success! The wonder of the ages! How many men had tried this same feat to no avail? And now I had solved the mystery of time travel in my own laboratory, with no one, save myself, to witness.

***

"Objection. Lacks foundation."

Judge O'Halloran had been carefully following the narrative, and he resented this useless interruption. He glared at Simpson, the young defense lawyer, whose stony expression seemed to deny that this matter had already been thoroughly debated in the pre-trial conference.

Fisk, the prosecutor voiced the judge's thoughts, but in a much whinier tone. "Your honor, we've already decided this in the hearing."

O'Halloran closely scrutinized Simpson, who stood, calmly waiting. His client, the Professor, also wore a detached expression, but as one who is resigned to his fate; the passive observer of another realm. Simpson had to know that he was being obstinate, and yet his expression was as cool as an ice-box.

"Your honor, reading my client's journal in this manner is a denial of his 5th Amendment right against self-incrimination."

"Overruled. The Court has already decided this issue. Your client took the option not to read his own writing, but the journal has been properly admitted."

O'Halloran nodded to the police sergeant, who sat in the witness box, and had been reading out of a bound leather journal. "Continue, sergeant."

The sergeant looked to the prosecutor. "From where I left off? I've lost my place."

Fisk shook his head, irritated. "Never mind that." Fisk walked back to the table and checked his notes. "Start from page 45."

Simpson stood up again. "Objection."

Fisk did not look up. "Goes to motive, your honor."

"Overruled."

The sergeant found the page in the journal and began to read.

***

It was today, when they buried my Janet, that I realized how low I had fallen. I held the umbrella over my dear Martha, as she clung closely to my side, shivering. The minister read from the Bible, promising new life to my Janet, but I felt lost. How long ago had it been? Five years?

I was doing well enough at the Edison Labs. I had made a name for myself, and I also earned a decent income. And then one day my doom arrived in the person of Mr. Price.

We had a nice apartment overlooking 4th avenue. I had been reading in my study, when Janet interrupted in her gentle way. She handed me the calling card of Mr. Price, who was presently waiting for me in the parlor.

How many times have I chided myself for ignoring my first impression: a corpulent, self-satisfied braggart; the loud voice, and vulgar mustache of a snake-oil salesman; the clammy handshake.

Of course he began by flattering me: my reputation preceded me; my achievements for such a young man.

"Let me come to the point. I wish to hire you away from your present position and provide financing for your own experiments." Mr. Price thought I was wasting my time in Edison's labs.

I was doubtful of any prospects with Price, but I tried to be tactful.

"Why am I willing to take the risk on an unknown, such as yourself?" Price chortled, and the Professor noticed a piece of cheese fall from Price's mustache. "You aren't exactly an unknown. You have two fairly profitable patents of your own. And there is your reputation at the Edison labs. Another former employee, Mr. Kroner, speaks very highly of your work."

Kroner! Another red flag, and yet I ignored it. I should have sent him packing the moment he mentioned Kroner. I remember the last time I saw him, walking out of the lab with an overstuffed carpet bag. He had been dismissed from the labs, and later it was said that he took several proprietary ideas with him.

And yet, I invited Price into my study, and we discussed business over cigars. Everyone has a weakness. Mine was a hunger for recognition of my talents, and for capital with which to finance my own experiments...

Soon I had my lab, and a larger home, with new furniture. Everything had been purchased from Mr. Price, who assured me I was getting a discount. He also provided the financing.

I would never quibble over such matters. I felt that the topic of finance was not the proper domain of a scientist. My father never discussed the prices of things in company. He considered discussing prices to be in bad taste. Father said that a man should ask a fair price, and that haggling was vulgar.

And I was left to my experiments. My greatest fascination was with Time. I had always wondered if its one-way course could ever be diverted. I had a vision in my mind's eye of that DaVinci sketch: a man, whose arms and legs were splayed about a circle, as though they were hands on a clock. I had always felt that the man in the clock was held bound by Time. I was curious to know if I could set him free.

My theory was that Time was held in place by gravity. If I could somehow remove the gravity from an object, a man would be free to travel backwards or forwards through time at a different rate...

***

"Objection! Relevance."

The prosecutor let out a sigh of exasperation. "Your honor, this explanation is necessary to understand the case."

Defense counsel Simpson was as calm as ever. "The Prosecution is spinning a fantasy, your honor. I don't know if the Jury can take much more of this."

"Let's try to keep the technical details at a minimum," the judge said.

The prosecutor nodded. "Yes, your honor. I assure you, we are only reading the abridged narrative." He turned to the sergeant. "Could you read from page 87?"

The Sergeant flipped ahead in the Journal. "Yes sir."

***

Two years slid past, and the venture had not yet shown any profit. I was called to Mr. Price's office.

"I'm thinking of dissolving the corporation."

"But you can't. I'm making such progress."

Price held up a handful of bills. "Progress? We haven't made a penny. Have you seen any of these?"

"I trust your management, Mr. Price."

"But these expenditures. I'm not able to sustain these by myself," he said. "If you were able to use some of the experiments from the Edison Labs, perhaps..."

"No. We discussed that. I promised Mr. Edison that I would not use any of his ideas. I signed a nondisclosure agreement."

Price shook his head. "Then I don't know what else can be done. I've had a lawyer draw this up..." Price reached into a drawer for a folder.

I was watching my chances at success disappear before my eyes. I was desperate. "Wait! How about my patents?"

Price stopped. "You want to sell them to me?"

"Yes. Could that provide financing for the corporation?"

Price put the folder away "For a time," he said.

There were many questions that the time machine presented. Would sending an object through time preserve the nature of the object? For example, the morning paper was, in the not too distant past, wood pulp. And before that, it was wood. If the newspaper were sent into the past, would it be transformed into its prior state?

Strangely, I was more concerned with the puzzle of how matter moved through time than I was with my own family. I watched as my new found wealth deteriorated. And my family was reduced to poverty.

My head was not for finance. I was at a loss to explain how Price was losing money, when I sold my house back to him for less money than I paid. My furniture was sold, and we moved into an apartment that was not as nice as the one I had lived in before I met Mr. Price. I had mistaken a line of credit for a salary, and after 5 years of hard work, I had nothing.

It was hard on all of us. But I supposed it was hardest on Janet. One evening Janet was bringing the food over to the table, and suddenly she fell... In my pursuit of fame I had missed the signs of her sickness. And then it was too late.

Price was good enough to pay for the funeral. At interest.

I was still in my mourning clothes when my experiments had finally paid off. Janet was not able to see my triumph. I had been able to send a newspaper forward in time 10 minutes. Ironically, the day's paper carried the story of Janet's sudden passing...

***

"Really, your honor is being too indulgent," defense attorney Simpson said.

The prosecution was setting up a large writing tablet with sketches on display for the jury.

"These sketches are necessary to understand the Professor's Journal," prosecutor Fisk said.

Simpson raised his voice. "They are manufactured evidence!"

"These drawings are *based on* the Professor's own drawings. They are merely done up large so that the jury may see them."

"Let the record show our objection." Simpson sat down.

The judge agreed. "Noted. Please continue."

***

Another curiosity involved the laws of probability. If an apple were to be sent backward in time, *but after the time machine had been created*, then the apple would have to appear in the time machine *before it was sent*.

The question then becomes: would the apple sent back in time then *exist at the same time as it was before it was sent?*

Now I was able to test the actual results of this hypothesis: *The probability of receiving something before it was sent depended on the certainty that I would send it in the future.*

I stood before the empty time machine, and focused on an apple on a tray. I firmly made up my mind to send the apple back in time, at some point in the future.

And then the apple appeared in the time machine.

I plucked the apple from the time machine, and sat it

down on the table next to its identical twin.

It was then that I saw the reverse side of the gravitational interplay with Time. I made to pick up the other apple, and found that it was substantially heavier. I made an effort to throw it, but I could not.

Gravity, it seems, served as a *guardian of time.* The apple that had not yet been sent back in time was preserved from destruction. Its fate could not be altered.

This became even more apparent as the time approached to send the apple back.

After placing the apple in the time machine, I watched myself literally moving without my own will. I watched myself push the buttons and pull the levers until the time machine made the apple disappear. Once the apple was gone, my hands ceased to be compelled, and they fell to my sides.

My decision to send the apple back in time *necessitated that I would be fated to send it.* And Gravity worked to make sure that the apple was sent.

One final experiment was provoked by my own desperation. I knew my chances of success were slim, but conscience demanded that I try.

Could I prevent my wife's death?

I set the controls, and then stepped into the time machine. I checked my watch.

I reappeared back in my lab, outside of the machine, several days before Janet collapsed. Unlike the experiment with the inanimate apple, there was only one of me. I found myself as I had been at that time: working in my lab. I was working on my experiments in the lab, but the motion of my limbs was not directed by my mind. As with the other experiment, I could only watch as I moved my limbs, as though I were a mannequin.

Once again I felt myself captured by Gravity, the guardian of time. For the briefest moment I might resist moving my hand, but then I was soon overcome and continued moving in the exact same way I had done several days before.

You cannot realize the utter helplessness of it all. The pattern had been set before in time: now that I had been sent back, my body was destined to repeat the same movements.

I watched my family move through the patterns they had made, like clockwork.

As the moment of Janet's passing approached, I knew I would be helpless to stop it. As before, Janet carried our dinner toward the table and then collapsed. I reached out for her, as I had before. Perhaps this time, I felt even more despair. I couldn't save my Janet. I could only relive my loss and compound my grief: The same way Price had found to compound interest on the debt I owed him.

As the past was proceeding toward the present, the moment that I had left, I began to feel anxiety over the realization of what lay ahead. That outcome was not at all determined. Certainly the past had been fixed: I had gone into the Time Machine and sent myself back.

But as I neared the point when I had sent myself back, I wonder if I would be sent back *again*? Would I step into the time machine again, and go back again and again? Would I be doomed to exist in an infinite loop?

My only chance was that time should move just slightly forward before I was thrust back again. I knew that the process was not instantaneous. I remember that when I sent the newspaper through time, there was a moment when the visual field flickered on and off. There was a moment of uncertainty at either end of a time shift. Would it be enough?

I watched as I set the controls on the Time Machine.

Then I was in the Time Machine, and I checked my watch. Again. I began to notice that the visual field flickered slightly, and that was when I attempted to break free.

I opened the door to the Time Machine and tumbled out just before the determining moment. There was a flash, but I was outside of the field!

After so many days I was free to move. I was in the present. I was free!

But I soon found that I was still in peril. I had allowed myself to be imprisoned by those spiraling debts. I was not able to properly care for myself and my daughter.

Now it was Martha's turn. She had grown pale and was running a high fever. Janet had always cared for our daughter. All I could do was worry.

I suppose at some point I became a desperate man. I was determined to set matters straight with Price. After a brief experiment, I knew I would be successful. I knew it as surely as I knew that I held his gold in my hands.

Once again I stood before his desk with my hat in hand. But this time, I was the one who had made a scheme beforehand.

I knew that Price would be immune to any pleas for charity for my sick daughter. "I appreciate your position," he said, "but surely you can't expect me to cancel your debt."

"But it's not fair. I've lost everything," I said. And this was true.

Price wiped his mustache, anxious to get back to the lunch I had interrupted. "We've both lost on this venture, my good man. It just happens that I could *afford* to lose."

"But I owe you money now," I said.

"You're blaming me because you spent money you didn't have."

"But my daughter is sick. She needs medical care," I pleaded.

"Children get sick every day," Price informed me. 'I paid for you wife's funeral already, and now you're putting the squeeze on me for your daughter? Do you confuse me for a charity?"

"No. But I thought ... we were partners."

Price stopped, and then reached down for a folder. "That's right. I didn't want to do this so soon after your wife's ... demise. But business is business."

"You want to dissolve the partnership?" I asked.

"Well it hasn't exactly been much of a success, has it?" Price opened up the folder, and slid the ink well over to my side of the desk.

"But it's finished!" I said.

"Finished? What are you talking about?"

"My Time Machine. I finished it. It's a success."

Price shot me a skeptical look, but then he put the folder away and invited me to sit down. "Can this be ... demonstrated?" he asked.

"Easily, yes." I took a gold coin out of my pocket and threw it on the table.

"Eh? What's that?" Price brought his fat hands together on the desk: hungry for the gold.

"That's a gold coin that I reckon is in your pocket right now," I told him.

"What? But how..." Price quickly reached into his pocket and pulled out a gold coin and laid it on the table.

"Examine them closely," I said.

Price pulled a magnifying lens from his drawer and looked at the coins. "They're exactly the same! They've both been shaved right there in the corner. How did you do that?"

"That coin, your coin, will be placed into my time machine and sent back to me exactly one hour ago. I know that it shall be done because the coin is here."

Price was rubbing his hands together, like a happy baby. "Remarkable. And this would allow things to go forward or backward in ... time?"

I nodded. "And people, yes."

"Remarkable." Price became quite animated and friendly now, and as we talked, I could see his eyes scheming. Confidence men trap their victims through the greed of the victim. It is greed that tells the fish to bite the morsel sitting on a hook. With Price, I knew that seeing two of his own gold coins would be enough.

We went back to my lab and I demonstrated the time machine for Price. First, the gold coin had to be sent back in time.

I knew that, even as I demonstrated this miracle, Price was reducing it all to the bottom line: how could he use the machine to make money?

Next I sent several gold coins forward in time. Ten minutes later, Price was clapping his hands as the coins arrived at where they had been sent. It was all too good to believe: here I was, demonstrating a magic money machine.

I told Price that I would not be able to use the time machine to make money, which was true. I told Price that I didn't have his head for figures. Which was also true.

And then I let price buy me out. Price drew up a contract, and then I received a fat check. And the partnership was finished. Shortly after I had cashed his check, he sent some workmen to my lab to take the machine away.

Price didn't have a curious mind, really. If it was simply a matter of scooping up gold, then why would I sell the machine to him? But he had been hooked by his own gold, and he was anxious to get more.

They were fated to be together. It had been determined by the time machine when it gave me Price's gold.

I didn't tell him the machine was evil: That I had spent five years searching for the secret to time, only to find it immutable. I didn't tell him because ... well, it was business.

Price would understand. He was a master of using time to create capital. Wasn't the interest on debt a function of time?

I wondered what he was scheming to do with the time machine? Investing in stocks that he knew were sure to rise? Staking out a mine before gold ore was discovered?

Would he research a map of gold discoveries? Or stock tables? How long had Price gone back in time? How long had he helplessly watched his life repeat without being able change its course?

Price had not stopped the time machine from resetting, as I had. He got stuck in the loop.

The fuse to Price's house blew out after 15 minutes, but for Price it must have been an eternity.

***

A deputy wheeled Price into the courtroom in a chair. Price was catatonic. He made nervous breaths with his mouth, and his eyes and mustache twitched. He seemed helpless and frightened, but he never would raise a finger.

"Look at him," the prosecutor said. "This captain of industry, reduced to a quivering, frightened animal."

***

I was called to Price's house by his staff, after they discovered his ... mishap. I took the opportunity to disable the time machine.

The jury acquitted me after the Prosecution failed to show how the machine could harm anyone. In its current state, the prosecutor could only cause the time machine to catch fire.

I suppose that I shall be held to answer one day for my crimes. And until then, I shall be confined to my number of years; an unknown number.

But until then I shall try to use my time more wisely. For I have learned that time can be a blessing ... or a curse.

The End.

9 THAT PERILOUS STUFF

Canst thou not minister to a mind diseased,
Pluck from the memory a rooted sorrow,
Raze out the written troubles of the brain
And with some sweet oblivious antidote
Cleanse the stuffed bosom of that perilous stuff
Which weighs upon the heart?

Lieutenant Bob Fellows was driving down the 126, just north of Los Angeles. He was nearing his exit, and he watched the activity of the farm just off the shoulder. There was a fairly ancient tractor, painted bright red, plowing. In the adjacent field, several men were picking fruit and laughing.

Lt. Fellows pulled off the highway, and drove down to what looked like a military compound and parked. He carried a dark brown attaché that had been a present from his wife. Fellows always wore his formal service uniform when he was making a house call.

As he moved through the compound, Fellows noticed a hand-painted sign that read, '*FORT NELSON*'. Fellows casually snapped a photo of the sign as he passed.

The grounds were well kept. There were several wooden barns that were cheerfully painted; two were red and white; one was yellow with a blue trim. Fellows snapped some pictures of these.

Rounding a corner, Fellows passed two men carrying shovels and a pick. Both were in civilian work clothes, jeans, and a loose fitting button up shirt, but both men saluted as they passed.

Fellows walked up the steps to the main residence: a large yellow craftsman home. The interior looked similar to a bed and breakfast, but there was no staff on hand for reception. Fellows stopped a man heading down the stairs.

"Pardon me. I'm looking for Pops Nelson. Would you happen to know where he is?"

The man saluted casually, even though he was not military.

"Yes sir. I believe Pops is out at number three. That's the maintenance shack. They've been having trouble with a tractor."

"Number three?"

"I'll show you. I'm going that way."

Fellows followed the man out to a small barn. Nearby he could see a tall, lean man talking very animatedly to the other men seated around a picnic table. All were dressed in casual working clothes, but the tall man stood up to salute Fellows as he passed. The other men noticed and did likewise.

Fellows gestured to the tall man, "Is that Pops?"

His guide laughed. "Oh no. That's Daniels. He's kind of the number two guy out here."

"Oh, Daniels. He's the one who wrote the letter to the congressman. He's the reason I'm here."

"That's Daniels for you. He gets things done."

Inside of number three barn, there was another, older

tractor with some men working on it. One of the men looked to be in his 70's, but still active and fit. He stepped back from the tractor, and shouted to the man in the driver's seat,

"Okay, Larry. Try cranking it."

The man on the tractor started the motor, but the tractor ran unevenly. There was a lot of black smoke.

The old man waved his hand excitedly. "Okay, shut it down. The mixture's way off."

Fellows' guide pointed out the older man. "That's him. The older fellow. That's our Pops."

Lt. Fellows approached Pops. Pops didn't salute.

"You must be Pops. I'm Bob Fellows from the Commission of the Honor Society. It seems that you've been recommended by Congressman Flemming as being a candidate for the Medal of Honor."

Pops shook Fellows' hand, but stared at him blankly.

"The who? I don't know what you're talking about son. I didn't do anything to merit any medal."

"I'm sure that's just humility on your part, sir. If you have some time, I would like to discuss your case."

Pops was already walking to the door. Fellows noticed that he walked with a slight limp. "Sure, we're late for lunch anyway," Pops said. "But I'm telling you, you've got the wrong man."

Fellows tapped his attaché. "We'll see about that."

Pops turned around and addressed the other men. "Let's all take lunch, fellas. Hey Nate, do you want to make sure the guys in the field come in and get something to eat?"

The man on the tractor, jumped down. "Sure, Pops." Nate dashed out of the barn.

Pops nodded towards where Nate had just disappeared. "He's only been here two weeks, but he's really doing well."

Pops and Fellows walked back out into the sunlight. There was a slight breeze, and Pops tugged at Fellows' sleeve. "Let's sit out here under these elms. I like to take my lunch out here. Have you eaten yet?"

"No, sir."

They had just sat down at a picnic table, when a man set a basket of sandwiches and sodas down in front of them, along with an ice cold water pitcher. "Daniels told me you'd be wanting these."

Pops smiled at the man. "Thanks, Doug."

Pops turned and waved to Daniels, who graciously bowed back.

"That Daniels. He's on top of everything, I'll say."

Pops grabbed a sandwich out of the basket. "You're going to like these sandwiches. Tom, the guy in the kitchen, used to be chef downtown."

Fellows opened his brief case and pulled out a file while Pops loaded up some plates.

Fellows clicked his pen and read off of the top sheet that was bracketed down to the inside cover of the file. "Now, you are Stanley "Pops" Nielson, correct?"

"Nelson, actually," Pops said. "No 'I'."

Fellows made a note. "I guess that's a typo. We were sent the most extraordinary letter by your Mr. Daniels, recounting your exploits in Viet Nam."

Pops had been opening a bag of chips, and stopped cold. "Oh dear. I think there's more than one typo here.... Lt. Fellows, I have to explain. Our friend Daniels has a tendency to ... exaggerate. I think my reputation has been grossly ... overstated."

"I don't understand."

"Why don't we do this. You tell me what your letter says I did, and then I will tell my version of the events."

"Fair enough." Fellows started to read. "In May of 1969 you were placed in charge of a batch of recruits at

Camp Pendleton....

'What am I doing here?'

Daniels found himself wondering this quite often in the past several weeks. Less than a month ago, he had been working in his uncle's hardware store. Everyone had to register for the draft, and when Daniels' number came up, there was no question of duty: he reported to the physical exam, and shortly after that, Daniels was boarding the bus to Pendleton.

It was there that Daniels first met Pops, their drill instructor. Pops was tough; all the instructors were. But Daniels and the others felt that they were very fortunate to have Pops. The men were all in agreement on this: beneath it all, they knew that Pops was their friend.

Daniels had run cross country in high school, so the three mile runs were easy for him. But not for everyone. There was one guy, King, who showed up to boot camp fifty pounds overweight. King had a hard time on the runs.

Other drill sergeants would ride a guy like King, and use him as a bad example. But Pops would never do that. Pops would leave the front of the pack and run back to get the straggler, inevitably King, and then he would encourage King to finish. Pops felt that it was important that all the guys started thinking of themselves as one unit. Everyone had to finish the run. Everyone had to come back.

It was not the usual practice, but after boot camp the front office decided to ship Pops out with the platoon. Pops had been in Vietnam several years before, so Daniels and the others had some added confidence that their leader possessed a greater understanding of what they would encounter there.

Shortly after arriving in country, a chopper had set their unit down into the field without incident. Daniels and the others spent their first evening sitting in a circle around Pops, who spoke to them like a football coach before the game.

"Now I know this is a dangerous place. And I know some of you are scared. Hell, I'm scared. Those people are tying to kill us." Some of the men laughed.

"But here's the thing, fellas. I've got this crazy idea. I'm not going to try and sell you on how many men you've got to kill, or how much ground we've got to take from the enemy." Pops paused here, and Daniels was curious to hear the plan.

"Here's the thing I'm going to try to do: I'm going to try and get everyone of you back alive. Every last one of you."

The men listened intently and nodded.

"Some people might think I'm crazy, but that's what I'm going to try to do. I'm going to try and get every one of you fellows out of here in one piece. But I'm going to need your help. You've got to promise me not to be reckless for yourselves, and you've got to keep an eye out for one another. Now do you think we can do that?"

The men nodded and looked around at each other. Daniels' eyes met those of the other men in the platoon: serious eyes staring out of lean faces that looked a lot less frightened than they had only five minutes before.

Daniels heard himself saying, "I think we can do it, Pops." And others joined in agreement. "Yeah, we can do it."

It started off with an impressive record of success. The platoon did not report any deaths or major injuries for six months of service. Pops led the men through every march, and there was no field or narrow into which Pops did not set his own foot down before anyone else.

Pops also looked out on the other end. One evening Daniels had heard Pops in a heated discussion with the Lieutenant about the proper method to approach an enemy target.

There was one time where they had come back from a march, and one man was missing: King. Pops shouldered his rifle and headed back out to the trail. Daniels felt the double rap on the top of his helmet, which was Pops' way of saying, "I am headed out to get King, would you like to come along?"

They found King after a few hours, and returned after dark, without one word of recrimination from Pops. King had been lost, and now he was found.

And then it all fell apart. They were under fire and the choppers came in to take them out. They were being sent out in groups of 12. There was a short dash to the Huey, where Pops was standing outside the last copter, shouting to the men. A burst ricocheted off the side of the Huey, and Pops motioned for them to get down. Pops crouched into a shooting stance, returning fire, while the rest of the men loaded into the copter. Daniels was the last one aboard, and he saw Pops get hit as he ran towards the Huey.

"Man down!" Daniels yelled. But the copter was coming under fire, and the pilot lifted off.

"Man down!" Daniels repeated. But the copter was already twenty feet in the air. Daniels grabbed his rifle and prepared to jump out when they got hit. There was a loud blast, and the copter pitched over sideways, and quickly smashed back down into the field.

Daniels scrambled from the wreckage. There was a lot of blood coming down into his eyes, and he felt dizzy.

There was smoke everywhere, and he could hear the zip of bullets passing by.

Although Daniels was able to make it to the edge of the forest, he was alone, with no weapon or food. The Viet Cong found him asleep, and Daniels was placed into a dugout prison cell, with bamboo poles for bars. As a punishment, he was forced to stand or kneel with his arms fastened to the poles above his head. The guards made sure to keep a steady drip of water on his head when this happened. Daniels felt himself going mad.

Rice was all he had to eat, and it never smelled right. On several occasions Daniels was led through a public square with other prisoners, bound together with leashes around their necks. People in the square would often spit and hurl abuse.

After several months in captivity, Daniels was in despair and had given up hope. Then he awoke in his cell to the sound of feet scrambling above.

"Hey Daniels!" A voice said.

Something dropped into the cell. Daniels couldn't see what it was, but he found it in the dark: a big fish. Daniels smelled it. It smelled good. It was raw, but it was delicious.

This continued on for several weeks. Fish were mysteriously dropped into the cell from above. Finally Daniels gathered up the courage to ask who his benefactor was.

"Hey, you. Who is it out there?"

The voice whispered back: "It's me! Pops!"

Daniels was overjoyed. "Pops? I thought you were dead."

"Not me. I'm fine. I've come back to make good on my word, remember? I'm going to try and get everyone of you back alive. Every last one of you."

"I remember, Pops."

"Now you sit tight, and leave everything to me."

Daniels smiled as he ate the fish in the dark.

One day when Daniels was tied up for torture, and the water began to drip down on his head, Daniels heard a sound system coming from far off. It was Chet Baker:

"Nights are long since you went away
I think about you all thru the day
My Buddy, my Buddy
No Buddy quite so true."

Daniels couldn't help himself. He burst out laughing, trying not to let the guards hear him. From up above, Daniels could hear that the guards were very upset.

Daniels laughed and sang along: *"Miss your voice ..."*

Then the escape came. There was an explosion above, and then shouting and gunfire.

Daniels heard the familiar voice: "Daniels! Get back to the wall."

Daniels backed away and looked up. There was a small explosion and then the bamboo grate was pushed down into the cell. A rope ladder dropped into the cell.

"Quick son! Up the ladder. We're making our break!"

Daniels scrambled up the ladder to find Pops, holding a very large machine gun.

Pops winked. "Quick like a bunny! We've got to get five clicks down stream to my hideout."

Daniels followed closely on Pops heels as they disappeared into the night.

No one had followed the pair as they made their escape in the darkness. At last, as the light broke forth,

Daniels and Pops came to an opening in the vegetation. Pops peeled back some branches to reveal a small hideout. Inside there was a small cot, bowls, and some books.

Pops set down his weapon, and made himself at home. "It's not much, but I call it home for now. We're going to stay here while I bust the others out, one by one."

"And then what?" Daniels asked.

"I'm going to steal a helicopter, and we're going to fly out of this joint. Meanwhile, there's a river nearby with plenty of fish."

Pops tossed a crude fishing pole to Daniels. "Now that I've got you, I can spend my time getting these other fellows out, and you can fish for a change."

Pops was sitting at the picnic table listening to Lieutenant Fellows finish Daniels' account.

"And one by one you and Daniels continued to rescue the men out of the prison. Finally, when you had enough men, you made a full assault on the prison and busted the rest of the men out. After that, you arranged for a helicopter to transport everyone back to safety."

Fellows finished reading the report, and handed it to Pops, who studied it.

"That's an interesting story," Pops said.

"Story? That doesn't agree with your version of the events?

Pops shook his head. "No, my version is not nearly as exciting."

"Of course, we expected that there was some hyperbole. Not much of Daniels' account matches up to our records, but that was part of the reason for my visit today." Fellows paused, waiting for Pops to elaborate. "So what happened in Nam?"

Pops shook his head. "I have no idea. I have never even been to Viet Nam. I've never been in the armed services."

"But our records show a Pops Nielson..."

"Yeah, but my name's *Nelson*. I spent the war in an office, working as an actuary." Pops shrugged his shoulders.

Fellows placed the report back into the folder. "I see."

"I have never fired a gun at another human being, and I don't ever plan to... No offense."

"None taken." Fellows thought for a moment. "Then how did you meet up with Corporal Daniels?"

"Well, I guess this goes back about fifteen years. I was working downtown. An actuary is kind of a boring job, but it pays the bills.

It was downtown Los Angeles. Pops wore a business suit and always brought his own lunch. He used to take his lunch to the park every day, and there were an awful lot of homeless.

Pops never would give money to the homeless. He would often wonder if he was just cheap, or if he felt like he would be throwing his money away. But even though he wouldn't give them money, Pops cared.

There was one homeless guy who really bothered Pops. This fellow never asked for change. He would sit by himself, and rummage through the garbage cans, talking to himself. It was Daniels.

Back then, Pops didn't know Daniels' name, but he was accustomed to seeing Daniels wearing the same dirty rags, mumbling to himself and regarding everyone with suspicion.

Pops couldn't stop thinking about Daniels. When Pops was eating dinner at home, he would wonder what

Daniels had found to eat out of the garbage can. He would even wake up at night and worry about Daniels.

One day, Pops saw Daniels eating garbage and thought, 'I've got a nice tuna sandwich here that my wife made for me. I'll bet he would like that sandwich.'

Pops walked up behind Daniels and left his lunch on the ground.

"Hey! I'm giving you this sandwich. It's okay. It's a good sandwich."

Daniels looked back and saw the lunch. Pops walked away, and Daniels opened the sack. Daniels scanned the area to make sure no one was watching, and then he began to eat the sandwich.

It became a pattern. Pops would start his lunch hour by finding Daniels, and then leaving him a lunch nearby. Pops knew that he couldn't feed all the homeless, but he could feed one of them.

Daniels would sometimes wake up from sleeping and find a lunch by his head.

And then one day, there was a minor miracle. Pops had left his lunch and was walking away, and from behind him, Pops heard Daniel say, "Thanks."

Pops turned around. Daniels was holding the lunch.

"Thank you for the sandwiches," Daniels said.

"Oh you're welcome son." Pops started to turn away. Daniels asked, "Are you Pops?"

Pops and his wife were never able to have any children, so he never had anyone call him 'Dad', or 'Pops', or anything like that. But he found that he liked it.

"My name's Nelson."

Daniels became excited. "Pops Nielson! You came back to get us out! Just like you said you would."

Normally Pops was a fairly meticulous person, but he didn't correct Daniels. He really liked his new nickname, and he didn't want to discourage it.

They started talking after that. Every day they had lunch together in the park. Pops would bring a little bag for Daniels, and they would discuss the events of the day.

After a few weeks, Pops decided that Daniels must be lonely and bored talking to himself, so he made Daniels a little gift of a radio. Pops remembered the look on Daniels' face when he took the radio out of the bag and turned it on.

The radio station was playing Chet Baker:

"Miss your voice the touch of your hand
Just long to know that you understand
My Buddy, my Buddy
Your Buddy misses you"

Daniels was overjoyed, and did a Chet Baker impression: *"Nobody quite so true…"*

Eventually, after he got to know Daniels, Pops fixed up a little room for him off the garage at his house, and Daniels came to stay with Pops and his wife. There was a single bed and some books. And, of course, the radio.

Daniels did chores around the house, and Pops paid him a little bit of money. Both Pops and his wife grew to be quite fond of Daniels.

And then Pops' wife passed away, and Daniels was the only friend he had left in the world.

Then Daniels got the idea of getting other homeless vets off the street. Daniels moved into the spare room in the house, and another homeless man moved in to the back room off the garage. That was Stevens. And then things started picking up steam.

Pops, Daniels, and Stevens built an addition onto the

house, and moved another vet into the garage. That was Wilson.

"By the time I retired, there was already a handful of veterans living with us. I cashed in my pension, and I sold the house and bought this farm."

Pops gestured around the grounds to Fellows. "And most of what you see here was done by the men. Daniels really runs the place. I just help out here and there. Every once in a while Daniels and some others go into the city and do what they call 'fishing', and they bring in another fellah off the street. There's always room for another one here. They act like this is some kind of a army base, but we don't keep any guns here. Just tools."

Fellows looked around at the compound. "Amazing. So this story of Daniels'...."

"I'm afraid it's mostly not what you and I would regard as the truth... But you have to recognize Daniels was going through some hard times when we met. I don't know how he remembers it all."

"And you were never in the military."

"No, sir. I never saw much use in fighting. But I must say, you trained these fellows awfully well. They do marvelous work here."

Fellows shook his head. "I'm afraid we can't take any credit for what the men have done here. I can't help but think ... we've let these men down."

Pops nodded sadly. "Well the war seems to do something to their heads."

"But you've rescued so many of them," Fellows said. "You brought them back... just like in the letter."

"Well we haven't rescued all of them, but we're working on it. The men are really doing all the rescuing, now."

Fellows got up to leave. "I guess I've heard enough."

"I'm very sorry to have wasted your time," Pops said.

Fellows stopped. "What waste? I'm writing up a recommendation for the medal, and I'm telling the story just the way you told it. You may not have fought anyone, Mr. Nelson, but I've never seen anyone single-handedly save as many vets as you have sir. And if that doesn't deserve a medal of honor, I don't know what does."

Fellows stood up straight and gave a salute to Pops, who was overwhelmed and didn't know what to do.

As Fellows walked back to his car, he passed Daniels who stopped and saluted. Fellows returned the salute, and then continued on to his car.

The End.

10 KING OF INFINITE SPACE

"O God, I could be bounded in a nutshell and count myself a king of infinite space, were it not that I have bad dreams."

Tom walked down Main Street, in Jefferson City, a block away from the Missouri river, and the abandoned shack where he had spent the night. All of Tom's belongings were tied up in a small bundle. He wore a pair of jeans and a sports jacket.

Tom stopped in front of the employment office and ran a comb through his hair. He breathed in deeply, and then forced his mouth into a smile before going inside. Tom had spent a lot of time thinking about what he was going to say: about the recommendation from the man at the gas station, and his eagerness to work... But the response from the receptionist was typically underwhelming: she handed Tom an application on a clipboard, and asked him to fill it in.

Tom used capital letters only to write his last, first and middle initial for what seemed like the thousandth time, while he wondered what circle of hell this was most like.

It wasn't long before he noticed Bud out of the corner of his eye. Bud was about Tom's age, similarly dressed, and had a perpetual grin. Bud made a short bow to Tom.

Tom stopped writing for a moment as he glanced up at Bud, and shook his head.

Bud sat down in the chair next to Tom's, and sighed. "Tom, this is not a good idea."

Tom continued writing while he spoke. "I knew you'd be along soon enough. Every time I start to get something good going on, you show up."

Bud made a pleading gesture with his hands. "Let's go back and hide out over in the mountains. It's still warm enough, and you've got enough money to last at least a couple of months."

"No offense, Bud, but I'm kind of getting tired of hearing myself talk all the time."

"Well you have me to talk to," Bud said.

"Same difference." Tom stood up and handed the application to the receptionist, and then sat down to wait.

"I'm telling you, this can't end well," Bud said. "People are going to find out about you."

"And then what?"

Bud recited Coleridge:

"And all who heard should see them there,
And all should cry, Beware! Beware!
His flashing eyes, his floating hair!
Weave a circle round him thrice,
And close your eyes with holy dread..."

Bud paused for a moment, and smiled. "Remember what happened with that radio station in Indiana?"

Tom waved his hand. "That was a fluke."

"This will be worse," Bud said. "You know what can happen."

Tom raised his voice a little louder than he meant to.

"That I might start getting a little respect for a change? Beat it Bud. You're just a figment of my imagination."

The door opened and Mr. Sims, a balding man in his 60's stepped out.

"Mr. Giordano?"

Tom stood up. "Yes, sir?"

Sims shook Tom's hand, and didn't seem to notice Bud. "Hi. Bill Sims. I've been looking over your application, and I noticed that you have a lot of experience with farm work?"

"Sure. I do all sorts."

"That's great. I've got an opening here, a family farm, just outside of town: Peggy Weaver. They had a hired man on there, but he had to leave town for some reason or another. They're not offering much pay, but there's room and board on top of that."

Tom smiled. "That sounds just fine, Mr. Sims."

Mr. Sims looked Tom over. "Like I said, it's not far out of town. I suppose you're on foot then?"

"I put a lot of miles on these feet," Tom said.

"Okay, then just stay on the main road north for about three miles. There's a small market. Take a right, and follow that road out to the Weaver place."

Later, Tom was walking away from town along the main road. He passed a large billboard with the picture of a Galaxy being connected up to a computer through a wireless network: "The Entire Galaxy at your Fingertips—Magellanic Broadband".

Peggy Weaver was a severe woman in her 50's. She and Tom were sitting in the Weaver living room, with the TV on in the background. Mrs. Weaver's face didn't give Tom much indication of whether she was pleased or disappointed.

"Mr. Sims says you have a lot of farm experience, so I

don't expect I'll have to explain everything. With our last hired man, I used to leave a list of chores tacked up in the kitchen. I'll feed you plenty, and I've always got a pot of coffee going."

"That'll be fine, Mrs. Weaver."

The TV in the living room was showing a rocket blasting off into space.

Peggy was distracted for a moment. "Oh, there's that billion dollar probe that was supposed to show us pictures of space... And then we didn't get to see anything."

The channel cut to showing highlights of the senate hearing. Senator Paulson was questioning a NASA scientist. Senator Paulson wore his spectacles perched on his nose. "And what was the cost of this Brontes rocket?" Senator Paulson asked.

The NASA scientist didn't even pause. "Two billion dollars, Senator."

"And this rocket was supposed to give us pictures of deep space, correct?"

"That's correct, Senator."

"And where are these pictures?"

"Well, we've been having some problems," the scientist began.

The Senator nodded. "It doesn't work, right? You spent two billion dollars on a piece of junk."

"I wouldn't say it doesn't work, but the photos are not the resolution we'd hoped."

The Senator had a cynical expression. "But you can't show the pictures to us?"

"Well, not yet. They're not for public consumption."

"Tell me the truth, Mr. Larson. This is a spy satellite isn't it?"

Peggy Weaver was upset by the television. "Two billion dollars on a piece of junk they sent into space. The government does nothing but waste our money and then scare us into giving them more." She turned back to Tom. "I'm sorry, Mr. Giordano. I'll have my daughter Miranda show you around the farm."

Mrs. Weaver called upstairs. "Miranda!"

Miranda poked her head down over the stair railing. "Yes, mother?"

Mrs. Weaver gestured towards Tom. "Could you show Mr. Giordano around the farm, and have him put his things in Carl's old room?"

"Sure, mother."

Miranda came down the stairs and smiled at Tom. She looked to be in her 20's, with light brown hair and glasses. Tom thought Miranda had a lovely smile. She nodded her head towards the door and he followed her outside.

Carl's old room was in a small guest cottage away from the main house. Miranda and Tom stood in the doorway. "This will be where you're staying. This was Carl's old room, but we cleaned up the place since he left. Carl wasn't the cleanest."

Tom walked inside, put his bundle on the bed and began sorting out his clothes into piles. "I'll try to be neat," he said.

"You don't carry much with you."

"I don't need much," Tom said. He took a pair of glasses out of the sack and put them on the desk. The frames were broken.

"Oh, your glasses are broken." Miranda sounded as if she were talking about a baby sparrow's wing.

Tom nodded. "That's okay. They're just missing a screw."

Miranda picked up Tom's glasses and inspected them. "They're wire frames, like mine. I've got an old pair up at the house. I can fix these for you in no time."

"That would be very nice of you. Thank-you."

Miranda walked out carrying Tom's glasses. "We're not paying you much, so I guess you could count this as part of our health and vision plan."

Just a moment after Miranda left, in walked Bud. "I don't like the looks of this," said Bud. "This never ends well. I don't know why women get so attached to you."

Tom was putting his things away, and didn't look at Bud. "It's all the wealth and power," he said.

"This is just going to hurt her, like all the rest. Let's pull up stakes now, Tom." Bud said.

"Leave it alone, Bud. You're making a big deal over nothing." But even as Tom said this, his wrinkled brow showed that he might be thinking the same thing.

Two weeks later, Tom was driving a tractor toward the barn. Miranda came running out from the house and waved for him to stop.

Tom parked the tractor and stepped down. Tom was wearing his glasses.

Miranda handed Tom an envelope of cash. "Mother told me to tell you that you should quit working and have some rest. This is your pay for the week. It's not much, but Mom threw in a bonus because she says you work awfully hard."

Tom folded the envelope and stuffed it in his shirt pocket. "Aw, she didn't need to do that."

"You deserve it, Tom. Anyways, Mom and I are going into town, if you want a ride."

"You two go ahead. I like to walk. Maybe I'll see you there."

Miranda smiled at him. "Okay. Suit yourself." She

154

ran back into the house.

The sun was setting as Tom walked toward the town, passing the Magellanic Broadband billboard.

Bud caught up to him. "So you got paid, I see." Bud said.

"Yep. I figure I'll go to town and get something to eat."

Bud jogged a little bit to match Tom's stride. "You might as well live it up while you can."

Tom frowned at him. "What's that supposed to mean?"

"Nothing. Say, Tom, do you mind lending me a couple samolians? I'm running a little low."

"Sure. Always glad to help out my imaginary friends." Tom handed a couple of bills to Bud.

"Thanks," Bud said. "Maybe I'll see you in town." Bud ran off, ahead of Tom.

Tom shouted after him, "Not if I.... Oh, forget it."

A few hours later, Tom was having a chicken fried steak, while the TV played on in the background.

The pretty blond news anchor had a serious expression.

"The first released photo from the Brontes space probe has caused quite an uproar today."

On the TV the news was a blurry photo of the Magellanic broadband billboard behind the Anchor.

"What appeared to be a photo of the galaxy was soon discovered to be an advertisement for an internet company. It is unclear at this time whether NASA is responsible for the photos, or whether this has been the work of a practical joker. Spokesmen from Magellanic Broadband have denied any knowledge of how the photos came to be picked up by the NASA satellite.

The news program showed Senator Paulson at a press conference. The anchor continued, "Senator Paulson, Chairman of the Senate Intelligence committee has called the released photos "a disgrace" and promises to look into any wrongdoing by the agency."

The TV news cut to a full shot of the Paulson press conference. Senator Paulson was speaking.

"If NASA is denying that they are using their space program for domestic spying, then why has their satellite beamed back a picture of a billboard on the earth? NASA has asserted that this is some sort of error, but I am still determined to get to the bottom of why they have stonewalled my committee for so long. Thankfully, we have worked out a deal. From this point forward, all data from the satellite must be made available in the form of a live feed. Which means that the satellite imagery from the Brontes will be available on the net 24/7...."

Tom had watched the report, and paid his bill in a hurry. He walked quickly through the dark town, keeping his head down, as if he were a celebrity trying not to be seen.

Bud sidled up alongside Tom. Bud was wearing sunglasses. "I guess you saw the news."

"Take those things off. You look ridiculous."

Bud kept his sunglasses on, and turned up his collar. "I'm trying to keep a low profile."

"Join the club."

"You never listen to me, Tom. And I think that's your greatest fault, seeing as I'm always right."

"Okay, so what now, smart guy?" Tom asked.

"Well, we don't take the main road, that's for sure."

Tom and Bud walked along a trail through the foothills that followed the main road. There was a lot of activity down below, and both men squatted down to reconnoiter.

There were several unmarked government cars parked nearby the billboard. Lights had been placed around the area, and some forensics people were taking measurements and photos.

Tom made a low whistle through his teeth. "Man, they work fast."

"It's a good thing for them you got your glasses fixed, otherwise that billboard would have been out of focus," Bud said. "It's only a matter of time now."

Tom shook his head. "Why does it always have to be like this?"

"Atlas had to carry the heavens as a punishment," Bud said.

"What did I do?" Tom asked. "Why would God do this to me?"

"Maybe it is a lesson in humility. Everyone has their cross to bear," Bud said. "Yours just happens to be the size of the universe."

Tom continued walking as he spoke: "But I can't control any of it. I can hardly even make enough to feed myself."

The next evening, Tom was laying on his bed. There was a knock on the door, and then Tom heard Miranda's voice.

"Hello?"

Tom sat up. "Yes?"

Miranda opened the door and poked her head in. "Mother and I are going to watch the meteor shower tonight. We wanted to know if you would join us."

Tom looked over to Bud, who was sitting on a chair behind the door. Bud shook his head "No".

Tom paused. "Uh, sure. What time?"

Miranda looked outside. "It's already starting to get dark. Say about 15 minutes?"

Tom nodded. "That sounds great."

Miranda smiled and closed the door.

Tom explained his thinking to Bud. "We can't leave until it's dark anyhow. At least this will give me an opportunity to say good-bye instead of just running out."

Later, Tom, Miranda and Peggy were sitting on the lawn in front of the Weaver home, having a picnic dinner. Peggy was filling up a plate for Tom. "I must say, Tom. We've never had anyone work as hard as you do."

Miranda sat next to Tom. "It's true, Tom. When Mother used to make up her list for Carl, he would never finish it. But you always end up doing even more than Mother can think of."

Tom's head was down. "Well, I've spent a lot of time doing this sort of work. It's all pretty easy when you know what you're doing."

Peggy looked through the basket. "Miranda, did you pack the pie?"

"Oh no, Mother. I'm sorry. I left it in the refrigerator." Miranda started to get up.

Peggy motioned for Miranda to sit, and stood up herself. "No worries. I'll get it. Be back in a jiffy." Peggy started back into the house.

After Mrs. Weaver left, Miranda said, "I'm kind of glad she left, Tom. I wanted to talk to you."

"I wanted to talk to you too," Tom murmured.

Miranda continued. "I don't want you to think badly of me. I don't usually do this, but I guess you've noticed that I kind of... liked you.... I don't usually talk to the hired men this way. In fact, I never... I just wanted to say that, if you wanted to ask me out, it would be okay with Mother, because I asked her.

Tom paused for a moment. "Listen Miranda, I like you too. But something's come up. I'm going to have to leave."

Miranda's voice took a hurt tone. "Leave? You just got here."

"I know. But I can't explain. I've got to go tonight.

Miranda turned away from Tom. "You're just like Mother said. You just want to wander around. Your type never puts down roots. You could never work a farm like this because you could never stay in one place long enough." Miranda ran inside the house.

Bud sat down at the picnic and grabbed a chicken drumstick out of the basket. "Real smooth, Tom. I don't think she hardly noticed, the way you eased out of that."

"Lay off, would you?" Tom said.

Bud finished the drumstick and threw the bone away. "We've got to go. They'll be all over this place tomorrow."

Tom stood up. "Let me at least say goodbye to Miranda."

Tom was walking through the kitchen of the Weaver home. He called upstairs. "Hello?"

Tom could faintly hear crying. Then he heard Miranda say, "I hate him!"

Peggy was consoling her. "Oh, honey. Calm down."

The TV in the kitchen was on, with the sound down. The anchor was sitting in front of a picture of Miranda, seen from Tom's point of view.

Tom looked over to Bud, who had also been watching the TV. They both turned and left.

Tom was in the bus station talking to the person at

the ticket counter. "You sure there's no more busses tonight?"

"Positive. The next bus out is to Kansas City at 7 a.m.," the clerk said.

"Let me get one for Kansas City, then."

Tom sat down in the lounge chair next to Bud. "I was just thinking: Why can't I just stay and tell them who I am? Why do I always have to run?" Tom was quiet for a moment. "How do I know it's even real?" he asked.

"What's not real? Do you think you're dreaming?" Bud slapped the armrest between their seats. "Feel that! That's reality, Tom."

"But how do I know that what I'm seeing on the TV is real?" Tom asked. "I see you, but nobody else does. Maybe the TV and the federal agents are all part of my imagination. Maybe I'm just crazy."

Bud raised his eyebrows. "Okay. Go ahead and turn yourself in. You know what will happen? People don't give up power. Once they see that everything, the whole world and all the stars are inside your head, they will use you to figure out how everything works... Of course some people would try to worship you like you were God."

"Like a god," Tom laughed. "Some god I'd turn out to be."

"But the people in power won't let that happen," Bud said. "They will keep you a secret. And then they will take you apart like a watch."

Tom thought about what Bud had said, and tried to sleep.

The next morning, Tom was standing in the doorway, looking out on the street. The clerk at the ticket window had said that the bus to Kansas City would arrive in about fifteen minutes.

Bud was standing outside the door, blocking Tom's way. "Just sit tight. Once we're on the bus, it'll be smooth sailing out of here."

"I know, Bud." Tom said. "I just want to stretch my legs. I've been cramped up all night."

Bud shook his head as he came back in the terminal. "It's risky." Bud motioned towards the TV in the waiting area. "Hey, you want to see if they got any more pictures of what you've been looking at, plastered all over the television?"

Tom stepped outside. "I'll be back in a second. I'm just going to stroll around a bit." Tom walked away, down the sidewalk.

"Vanity of vanities, and all is vanity," Bud said.

Tom was walking in front of an electronics store. On the TV inside, there was a shot of Miranda behind the news anchor. On the side of the street opposite Tom, there were a couple of men in suits, wearing sunglasses with earpieces.

Bud sidled up to Tom. "We've got to amscray. This place is loaded with the G-Men. If they had your profile, they'd be picking you up right now."

Tom turned his back to the street, and spoke in a low tone. "I just wanted to see what was happening."

Tom was watching the TV in the shop:

The anchor read a new announcement.

"The latest word from NASA is that they will be broadcasting a live feed of their transmission, in an effort to see how it has been interrupted. We will be going to that live feed any moment."

On the TV, there was a blank. Then the TV switched to an effect much like that of a mirror reflecting another mirror. There was a TV screen, showing a smaller TV screen, and so on, ad infinitum.

Bud said, "Don't look away, now Tom. If they see this street, we're pegged."

Tom stared directly ahead, into the TV. "What do I do?"

"Just stay focused on the TV," Bud said. "They'll turn it off in a second. It looks like an error."

The TV cut back to the Anchor. "I'm sorry, ladies and gentlemen. There appears to have been some technical error, and we're trying to work out the details."

Tom didn't look away from the set. "What now?"

Bud pulled out his sunglasses. "Put these on."

Tom put them on. "I can't see a thing."

"Yeah, I inked out the lenses. Let's get back to the bus stop."

Tom and Bud walked away from the shop just as the TV cut away to another live feed. This time the screen went totally black.

Tom tried to walk casually.

Bud spoke in a low tone: "We're passing some G-Men right now. Here's your chance to turn yourself in. If they arrest you and torture you, then you'll know for sure you're not crazy."

Tom didn't answer.

Bud said, "No takers? Okay, then just keep going straight. There's a curb coming up in about twenty feet. I can see the bus pulling in right now."

A few minutes later, Tom was riding away on the Bus. Bud was in the seat next to him. Tom tapped the glasses. "When do you think I can take these off?

"I don't know, Tom. I figure our best chance is to avoid any landmarks."

"Living outside again," Tom said

"Living off the land," Bud said boldly.

Tom was less enthusiastic. "Yeah. Living off the land."

The End.

11 FIT FOR TREASONS

The man that hath no music in himself,
Nor is not moved with concord of sweet sounds,
Is fit for treasons, stratagems, and spoils.

I.

The docent was a typical debutante: cheerful, with loads of social grace, and perhaps a little overly sentimental. Judging from the 20 or so students following her through the Smithsonian Aero-Space Museum, she was pretty good at telling stories. The group stopped in front of a display case holding a steel-encased book. The book lay open to a random page: its casing was dented and battered, and the pages were singed as though they had escaped a fire.

"Okay y'all, this next display is called the Leitmanov diary. I have to tell you, this is my favorite display in the whole museum. Now you might be wondering why we have a book in the Aero-Space Museum. Does anybody have any guesses?"

A small boy with big glasses raised his hand, and the docent nodded for him to ask. "Was the book from outer space?" he asked.

The docent smiled and nodded. "Kind of. It did go out into space. Does everyone remember the Nautilus Explosion?"

Some of the children raise their hands.

The docent continued, "Well a few years ago, one of our space ships had an explosion in space. Our space scientists were not able to find out what caused the explosion because everything... well it all blew up. And then when the space ship went into re-entry, that's when it comes back into the atmosphere, the ship got really hot and burned up."

The docent pointed to the book. "See how busted up the book is? Well that's because the book got hot during the re-entry. Does anyone notice anything else about the book?"

A little blond girl didn't raise her hand. "The writing is all strange. It's not in English."

"That's right. That's Cyrillic. Does anyone know what language that is?"

There were no hands.

"Well that's what the Russian language is written in. I didn't know that either. It seems Mr. Leitmanov, the man who wrote the diary, was a Russian Professor who was invited to join the United States Space Program as a goodwill gesture. And after the spaceship blew up, nothing was left from the ship except this diary. So the Scientists looked at the diary to find out what caused the explosion. And do you know what they found?"

The docent's eyes got watery at this point. She dabbed her eyes with a handkerchief.

"Excuse me. I always get choked up here. What the scientists found was that Mr. Leitmanov had just written poetry... to his wife. It was just love poetry that he was quoting, written by a famous Russian named Pushkin. Isn't that beautiful?"

166

All of the children nodded. Some of the girls started to weep like the docent.

The docent went on, despite her copious tears. "I was lucky enough to meet Mrs. Leitmanov about a year ago..."

A year earlier the docent was posted at the information desk near the entrance of the Aero-Space Museum when a pale blond woman came up to the counter.

"I believe you have something that belongs to me," the woman said.

The docent had smiled. "And what would that be?"

The blond woman gestured to the display case. "That book over there is my husband's diary. I am Mrs. Leitmanov."

Phone calls were made, and soon Mrs. Leitmanov was accompanied by the docent and Colonel Sharp to a plain, empty office. The docent was pushing a small aluminum cart that carried the steel-cased journal. The docent took the journal off the cart and placed it on a table.

Colonel Sharp was the museum's public relations manager. "NASA is only too willing to let you read your husband's journal, Mrs. Leitmanov. You know, we already have it transcribed in Russian and English?"

Mrs. Leitmanov nodded. "Yes, Colonel. I just wanted to see my husband's writing one last time. You understand?"

Upon hearing this, the docent started to get choked up, and silently dabbed at her eyes with a handkerchief.

Colonel Sharp's face displayed compassion. "I understand. Well, it looks like you have everything you need here. If NASA can be of any further assistance, please let us know."

Colonel Sharp held the door open for the docent, and

then followed her out, closing the door behind them. Mrs. Leitmanov sat down at the desk and opened the Journal to the very beginning. Her fingers followed along the Cyrillic text.

"Sad reveries are swarming in my over-burdened soul,
And Memory before my wakeful eyes
With noiseless hand unwinds her lengthy scroll."

Vladamir Leitmanov was 40, tall, thin, with thinning blond hair that was turning gray. He sat across from the Minister of State, who was a heavy-set man with thick brown hair and a stoic expression.

"Why me?" Leitmanov said.

"Vladimir... Don't be modest," the minister said. "Your book on physics is world famous. And you were requested specifically by the American State Department. Who are we to deprive them of the famous Leitmanov?"

It was spring, and Leitmanov and Mrs. Leitmanov were walking down a pleasant garden path lined with blossoming cherry trees.

Leitmanov was reciting poetry.

"And, caressing me, she said:
'Preserve this talisman, my love,
In it power is hidden!'"

Mrs. Leitmanov corrected him. "In it *secret* power is hidden!"

"In it *secret* power is hidden!" Leitmanov repeated. "My love has made it thine."

"You must concentrate," she said.

"I am concentrating." Leitmanov moved to kiss Mrs. Leitmanov. She moved away.

"Please..." she said.

"How can you speak poetry on a beautiful day like today and not *feel* it?" Leitmanov said. "Can't you feel it stirring something in you? In me, when I hear Pushkin, it's like music. How I wish you could feel this music."

Leitmanov caressed Mrs. Leitmanov's cheek.

In the office at the museum, Mrs. Leitmanov unconsciously touched her cheek while reading the book...

It was 105 degrees at the Astronaut Training Center in Houston. Leitmanov was walking across the practice field, dressed in a t-shirt and shorts and trainers. He shook hands with a man wearing camouflage pants, sunglasses, and hair that was cut high and tight.

"Professor Leitmanov. Welcome. I'm Colonel Zeke Lewis. I'll be in charge of this little outing."

"Thank you, Colonel," Leitmanov said. "I'm glad to see someone of your vast experience will be leading."

"My success is only due to the great people I get to work with." Col Lewis pointed to a knight chess piece that Leitmanov was wearing on a chain around his neck. "You play chess?"

"I dabble," Leitmanov said.

"We should play sometime. Let me introduce the other crew members."

Behind Col Lewis, an informal line of men and women stepped forward to greet Leitmanov: Captain Brad Harmon was Lewis' co-pilot; Major Katrina Walker was the flight surgeon; Angela Baxter would be working with Leitmanov and performing several physics experiments; and Ward Taylor would be taking along several live specimens for zero gravity testing.

Lewis addressed the crew: "Ladies and gentlemen, we

are all going to be working closely together for about six months. From this point are we are a team: inseparable. We are going to live as a team, and work as a team.

Leitmanov took in each crew member's face as Lewis made his speech. Pushkin's words came back to him:

"I remember the wonderful moment of our meeting
you appeared before me like a fleeting vision,
An angel of beauty and purity"

There followed weeks and months of exercise and training. Leitmanov worked closely with the other crew: doing sit-ups with Harmon, and daily running with Angela Baxter.

One day Leitmanov was in the kitchen, taking a pill out of a prescription bottle and swallowing it, just as Dr. Katrina Walker came in.

"Whoa, Vladimir. I don't mean to be nosey, but this medication wasn't on your chart."

Leitmanov waved this aside. "Oh, it's just for my stomach."

Dr. Walker held out her hand. "Do you mind?"

Leitmanov handed Katrina the bottle. She read the label.

"Is it serious?" she asked.

"No. I just take this when I have heartburn," Leitmanov said. "Is this going to be a problem?"

Dr. Walker handed back the bottle. "Let's just keep this between ourselves. Command wants to know everything going aboard the flight. You know, weight and all that."

Leitmanov nodded. "Right."

Leitmanov started out, and he heard Dr. Walker say, "By the way, if you run out, the generic's a lot cheaper."

"Thank-you, Doctor." Leitmanov said.

The entire crew met at a bar to celebrate the end of their training. Col Lewis was seated next to Leitmanov. Lewis held up his glass of beer to toast.

"This is to the best crew I've ever had the pleasure of working with. May our camaraderie continue to grow as we move into space, so that we can prove an example of international friendship."

Everyone cheered, and clinked their glasses.

Col Lewis noticed Leitmanov's glum expression. "Gee, Vlad, why the long face? You worried about the mission?"

Leitmanov started, as if he had been woken up. "What? No, actually, it is... it is my wife. She is... going to have a baby, and I forgot to call."

"A baby! That's big news. When is it due?"

"Very soon. That is why I wanted to call. It might come while we are in space. I was going to call, but I forgot my phone."

Col Lewis pulled out his cell phone. "Here you go buddy."

"It is to Russia. I think that is a toll call."

Lewis waved his hand. "Forget about it. We're comrades, right?"

"Yes. Comrades. Thanks, Zeke. You are a good friend."

Leitmanov dialed as he walked away from the table. He spoke in Russian: "Hello, Anna? I am using a friend's phone. How are you? Not yet? Okay, my love."

Lietmanov started reciting Pushkin:

"In the weary boredom of the world,
A gentle voice kept sounding in my ear,
And in my dreams I saw your delicate features..."

In the museum office, Mrs. Leitmanov stared at the page in the book and compared it to another page that she brought with her. On her own paper she began to circle individual words, and underline others.

The crew were in the launch area, getting suited up for the flight. Leitmanov got a call on his cell.

"Hello?" He listened for a moment, and then shouted to his crew mates. "It is a boy! I am a father!"

The crew shouted out congratulations. "Way to go Vlad!" said Col Lewis.

On the other side of the phone, Mrs. Leitmanov said,

"Years passed in a riotous rush.
And former dreams lay scattered,
and each year I forgot your tender your voice,
And how heavenly your features to me seemed..."

Mrs. Leitmanov was copying from the journal. She noticed a drop of water falling onto the page. Mrs. Leitmanov wiped a tear from her eye.

Inside the space ship, Harmon entered Leitmanov's cabin.

"Bad news, Vlad. We're going to have to take a temporary detour. There's some minor repairs that we need to make on a satellite."

Leitmanov nodded and continued writing into his journal.

Leitmanov was wearing a space suit, outside of the ship. All he could hear was the sound of his breathing apparatus. Leitmanov used a small rocket thruster to speed towards a large satellite.

Behind him, outside of his view, another figure was

leaving the space ship.

Inside the motel room, Mrs. Leitmanov woke up out of a bad dream. She wiped her eyes and looked at her watch: It was 3:23am.

Mrs. Leitmanov arose, and took out her journal notes. She laid them on the motel desk. Mrs. Leitmanov took the cap off her lipstick case and unscrewed the base. She removed a small notebook that was concealed inside the lipstick case.

Using the notebook, Mrs. Leitmanov began to make notations on her journal.

II.

It was back at the time when Leitmanov sat before the desk in the office of the Minister of State.

"So I am to be a spy?" Leitmanov asked.

"It's for a good cause..." the minister said.

"I just hate being underhanded. I have always tried to be straightforward with people."

The Minister shrugged his shoulders. "Try to think of it as a game."

It was during the training phase in Houston. In Col Lewis' office, Lewis and Leitmanov were playing chess. Lewis was eying the board intently.

Leitmanov noticed a ring on Col Lewis' hand. On Lewis' desk was a picture of Lewis and Harmon in Air Force Uniforms.

Lewis moved his queen. "Check."

Leitmanov studied the board for a moment, and then moved his knight. He spoke briefly in Russian, and caught himself, shaking his head. "I think that is checkmate."

Col Lewis studied the board for a moment, and then

laid down his king.

Suddenly, Lewis let out some colorful language, and swept the pieces from the board. As suddenly as the storm rose, it vanished again. Col Lewis looked bashful. "Sorry about that. I really thought I had you," Lewis said. "Now I see why you wear that pendant. You really know how to use the knight."

Leitmanov bowed his head. "Thank you. I used to enjoy this game more. Now I find it is so much memorization. All the moves and strategies have been formulated and written about. Nowadays you can read a few books and suddenly you're a chess master."

"That's what I did, I'm a afraid," Lewis said.

"Don't be hard on yourself," Leitmanov said. "I'm sure when it comes to the game of life, you are a formidable challenge."

In her motel room, Mrs. Leitmanov was transcribing from her notebooks. She took a sip of coffee and rubbed her eyes.

The Minister of State showed Leitmanov a desk with the knight pendant on a chain, the lipstick case, and some other gadgets. "We have several tools to help you avoid detection."

Leitmanov held up the knight pendant and examined it closely.

The Minister extracted the small notebook from the lipstick case and held it up. "We've arranged a code for you," the minister said. "It's based on Pushkin."

"Pushkin?" Leitmanov asked.

"Yes, that is why you were the perfect choice. Your knowledge of Pushkin is legendary. By substituting key words we have created a nearly indecipherable code. Anyone else might think you have made a mistake and forgotten a word."

At the bar, Leitmanov was using Lewis' phone, speaking in Russian. "I am using a friend's phone. How are you? Not yet? Okay, my love."

Mrs. Leitmanov sat in the Minister of State's office, listening on the other end of the line. Nearby, a clerk was listening in headphones, and writing in Russian: "Track this device. I believe this is the ring leader."

Mrs. Leitmanov spoke in code, in Russian: "We are getting the information off now. We will call back, and you can download the frequency they are using."

The next day, at the launch area, Leitmanov was listening at his phone, hearing about the birth of his son. This is the coded message he heard Mrs. Leitmanov say: "At 21:30 send a cable to the ship from your transmitter. It will order Lewis to rendezvous with the Satellite."

Inside the space ship, Leitmanov unscrewed the knight chess piece pendant, and removed a transmitter. He pushed a small lever.

At that moment, Lewis and Harmon were at the controls of the ship. Lewis got a signal on his earpiece and wrote it down.

Lewis made a signal to Harmon, and Harmon pushed a button, which shut down the camera and microphone that were recording their actions.

"We have to go by the Store," Col Lewis said.

Harmon nodded. "What's wrong?"

"Small repair. Shouldn't be more than a few hours. Let everyone know we're taking a small detour."

Harmon left Leitmanov's cabin after telling him of the Detour. Leitmanov wrote in code in his journal:

"They have taken the bait. Now I have to get to the satellite first."

Back in the Minister of State's office, the minister was holding out Leitmanov's vial of prescription pills. "It's a very potent gas that will render everyone unconscious."

Inside the galley of the spacecraft, Leitmanov was wearing a breathing apparatus and inserting his medication into the ship's air supply. It was timed to give Leitmanov about two hours to get to the satellite alone.

Leitmanov took longer than he expected getting into the space suit. He had less than an hour to destroy the satellite.

III.
Back in the Minister of State's office, the Minister had motioned towards a leather chair. "Have a seat, Vladimir."

Leitmanov sat down. The Minister turned off the lights.

On the wall was a slide presentation. There was a distant picture of the satellite.

The minister said, "This is Satellite X274. NASA states that this is a communications satellite, but we've noticed that there is very little communication being sent to it. And it doesn't appear to be used to relay information. Rather, a few messages are sent to it and it occasionally transmits."

"What is it?" Leitmanov asked.

Another slide showed a blurry appendage of the satellite.

"We think it is a high powered laser." The Minister pointed towards a cylindrical piece. "This bit right here is believed to be a cannon capable of taking out a small city."

"You're joking," Leitmanov said.

"I wish I was."

"Is that legal?"

The Minister shook his head. "No. It is against International Law."

"What about the Ambassador?" Leitmanov asked.

"Diplomacy won't help here. The United States doesn't know about it either."

Leitmanov was incredulous. "They don't know about their own satellite?"

Another slide showed an Egyptian 'Amenta' symbol of the Underworld.

The Minister said, "We believe the government of the United States is under the control of a secret organization. This symbol might be used to help them recognize their own members."

Leitmanov and Col Lewis were playing chess in Col Lewis' office. Lewis was debating a move, and Leitmanov was staring at Lewis' ring. Along the edges of the crest, he could see engraved the small Egyptian symbol of the underworld.

Col Lewis moved his queen and said, "Check."

IV.

Colonel Sharp was reading email at his desk when he heard a sharp knock.

"Enter," Sharp said, without looking up.

A young lieutenant poked his head in. "Sir, I've encountered a strange anomaly. Maybe it's a mistake, but..."

"What is it?" Sharp was known to be impatient just before lunch time.

The lieutenant came into the office. "I was printing out a copy of the temporary transfer of Leitmanov's Journal. You know. For the record?"

"Yes?"

"I wanted to put a picture of his widow into the file. So I downloaded her picture, and this is what came out."

The Lieutenant laid a printed portrait down on the desk. It was of a middle aged woman with brown hair.

"That's not Mrs. Leitmanov."

"That's what I thought. So I used the computer to check the Russian papers."

The Lieutenant laid another printed story on the desk. It showed a picture of Leitmaov getting an award. He pointed out the relevant passage for the Colonel to see.

"It says Leitmanov is a widower," the Lieutanant said.

"Maybe he got remarried," Col Sharp suggested.

"Maybe he did. But I couldn't find it in any newspaper."

Col Sharp examined the papers on his desk. "If this is Leitmanov's wife, then who is reading his journal?"

A year before, back in the park, Leitmanov and the ersatz Mrs. Leitmanov were walking together.

"Can't we spend some time together just to ourselves?" Leitmanov said.

"There is no spare time," his companion said. "We have our mission."

"Our mission." Leitmanov sighed. "Right now I don't care a fig about the mission."

"That's just hormones," the lady said. "It will pass."

Leitmanov embraced *Mrs. Leitmanov*. "You're telling me you don't feel anything?" he asked.

Her eyes were cold. "We've been walking through this beautiful park, in springtime, reciting Pushkin. If you didn't feel *something* there were would have to be something wrong with you. But that doesn't make it love. Love is something different."

Leitmanov gazed down into her eyes. "But don't *you* feel anything?"

In the motel room, Mrs. Leitmanov was drinking some coffee, remembering back to that day in the park, hearing her own voice. "I don't *let* myself feel anything," she had told him. "It's just poetry. It doesn't mean anything. Think about the code."

Colonel Sharp and the lieutenant opened the door to the museum office where Mrs. Leitmanov had been decoding the journal. The office was empty.

The docent was standing behind the main counter of the museum when she saw Colonel Sharp and the Lieutenant approach in a hurry.

Sharp didn't waste any time on a greeting. "The widow ... Mrs. Leitmanov. Do you know where she is?"

The docent shook her head. "She didn't come in today. I think she finished reading the journal."

The Colonel turned on his heel and headed back to his office, followed by the lieutenant. He spoke in hushed tones to the lieutenant. "Get the FBI on the line ASAP."

Leitmanov was in a space suit. He had made it to the satellite and was currently tearing apart a circuit board.

Another figure in a space suit was approaching him from the ship. Leitmanov could hear Col Lewis through his headphones in the suit.

"Stop it, Leitmanov. Back away from the satellite!"

Leitmanov continued working. "You're too late. The Satellite is permanently disabled."

"You couldn't have finished that fast," Col Lewis said.

"It is a lot easier to break things than to fix them," Leitmanov rejoined.

Col Lewis saw that Leitmanov was still working. "I said stop working!"

"The game is over," Leitmanov said. "Checkmate."

Lewis fired a laser that nearly hit Leitmanov, but Leitmanov continued to work.

"I say when it's over," Lewis said.

"Stop it you fool!" Leitmanov said. "This cannon still contains plasma."

"So it's not too late?" Lewis fired another shot, hitting the wrench Leitmanov was holding, and knocking it out of his hand.

"The Canon is permanently disabled," Leitmanov said. "It cannot be repaired, but it is very dangerous!"

"Why should I trust you?" Lewis asked, firing again. Again, he missed.

Leitmanov regretted that he had not taken a laser from the ship. "Stop it! You'll destroy us all!"

"I'll destroy you." Lewis fired again, and the laser passed through Leitmanov, killing him.

Lewis continued toward the Satellite.

Suddenly, something popped off of the satellite. Lewis regarded this for a moment, and then continued on his path.

Then the satellite exploded.

A small piece tore through Col Lewis, killing him instantly. Another larger piece hit the space ship. And then the space ship exploded.

Near Muleshoe, Texas, a farmer was plowing a field, and listening to Pink Floyd in his air conditioned tractor.

Suddenly, a meteor streaked through the sky, and

crashed down a hundred yards in front of the tractor. The farmer jumped down, and ran to see the crash site.

Not long afterward, a dozen FBI appeared and cordoned off the farm.

Years later, Mrs. Leitmanov was in the motel transcribing the journal. She could imagine Leitmanov's voice as she wrote:

"I am writing what could be my final entry. I do not think that I shall be returning from this mission."

Leitmanov had been writing this last passage just before the ship had altered its course towards the satellite.

"Col Lewis will not let me survive once he finds out what I have done," he wrote. "He is the type that turns over the chessboard. Ah, we cannot pick our enemies…"

In the motel room, Mrs. Leitmanov checked her watch, writing as quickly as she could.

"You remember, Anna, in the park, you told me it was "only poetry" and that I must think of the code. I wonder what you must think of this: I am transcribing a poem within the code. It is a love poem to you."

Mrs. Leitmanov took a deep breath. It was difficult for her to fight back the tears as she transcribed.

"Here I am,
as far from you as two human beings have ever been.
But still I feel myself drawn back to you.
I am in the vast coldness of space,
but my heart still beats warm, for you…"

Leitmanov was in his space suit, letting himself out of the ship, but what he had just written was still very clear in his mind.

"And though I am sure that I shall soon be even further from you,
separated by death, I feel brave."

As Leitmanov approached satellite, he had a broad smile upon his face. It was as though he alone knew the punch-line to a very funny joke.

"Because I know you would want me to be brave.
Is it poetry or is it code?

"The heart beats in ecstasy,
Old joy is resurrected;
By God and inspiration
Of life, and tears, and love."

In the motel parking lot, Colonel Sharp and two FBI agents stepped out of an unmarked FBI car. They rushed over to room 12.

One of the FBI agents broke the automatic lock on the door, and the three of them stepped inside the room. It was empty.

At last, Mrs. Leitmanov was standing before the desk of the minister of state.

"Leitmanov sent us a signal from the satellite notifying us that he had disabled the cannon," the Minister said. "That was shortly before the ... accident. The satellite was completely destroyed. The mission was a success."

"I'm sure Valdimir would be pleased," Mrs.

Leitmanov said.

The minister nodded. "Leitmanov was a great man. He was an old friend. We went to school…"

A tear started working its way down Mrs. Leitmanov's cheek.

The minister continued. "The bureau appreciates your … candor in allowing us to read his last poem to you."

"I was proud to show it off," Mrs. Leitmanov said. "To be loved by such a man."

Inside Col. Sharp's office, Sharp and a general were having a conference.

"In the end, we decided that, if there had been a code in the journal, that horse is out of the barn, so to speak," Sharp said. "It has been sent to the intended target."

"And what is the journal's status now?" the General asked.

"Naval Intelligence is still working to crack the code, but outwardly it's a matter of damage control," Sharp said. "We'll leave the Journal on display with the same cover story: a collection of love letters from a brave astronaut."

"If they only knew," the General said.

In the museum, the docent was taking another elementary school class on the tour. "Okay y'all, this next display is called the Leitmanov diary. I have to tell you, this is my favorite display in the whole museum..."

The End.

ABOUT THE AUTHOR

Henry Garon is an attorney living in San Diego. He likes to barbecue and swim.